TWISTED REALITY

NDO IME UDOH

Editor: Gloria Ogo
            GO EDITS Polished Manuscripts

—

DEDICATION

I dedicate this book to my beautiful daughter, Divine, and my parents, Mr. and Mrs. Butler, my strength and the reason this work is a reality despite all odds.

APPRECIATION

All glory to the Almighty God, the giver of ideas and capabilities. I thank my editor, Ms. Gloria Ogo, GO EDITS Polished Manuscripts, for polishing my story in a magnificent way.

I also thank all members of my family for believing in me. Especially my mother Mrs. Stella Butler, who encouraged me to publish this book, my elder sister, Mrs. Catherine Ewah, author of *Basic Steps to Success*. She is a huge inspiration all the way.

My last sister, Ms. Etini Udoh, a great poet, is the muse behind my storytelling gift, reading her writings motivated me to put the stories in my head on paper.

The light shines in the dark, and the dark can never extinguish it.

- Holy Bible; God's word translation.

INTRODUCTION

Twisted Reality has its character come much alive to its reader.

You will love, hate, fear, remember and even become them.   Ndo's theme focuses on the message that your next decision might make or break you. She offers hope that no matter the depth of darkness, a greater light reveals the shadow and secrets of the hidden places.

Then there is a twist of deadly romance between light and darkness, and its outcome is nothing short of horror.

CONTENTS

CHAPTER 1

Single for almost three years, I learnt a lot about my sexuality. I discovered a prowess hidden all these years. The urge broke to the surface of late, and edged me on to confront a romantic side of me I never knew existed.

In front of the full-length mirror, I peered at my face, admiring my new skin glow.

"Oh, yes!" I murmured, my fingers trailed my red lips. "Next relationship will be mind-blowing romantic and, of course, adventurous." I winked at my reflection and a slow smile crept up my face.

The new guy's name was Mike. I bumped into him at The Church Of The Angels, while at a colleague's wedding. After the first hello, sparks flew, newly-found-friend mood activated, and we became pen pals. I never knew I had a flair for writing until we began to exchange love notes daily, though we lived in the same part of town and visiting each other would be a piece of cake.

I wanted to take it slow but the more I resisted, the greater the tug. My heart raced each time I mentioned my desire to meet him in my letters. Something fluttered in my stomach, which could be the proverbial butterflies.

My notes went deeper than mere words. I bled my heart on those pages, unveiled experiences I would love to experiment on when we met. My urge to have him inside me was so intense, I went wild describing the depths of sexual conduit we would soon ravish on each other. I let him know I wanted my legs to hang on his shoulders while he rammed me like a boss. Call me crazy, but I listed the aphrodisiac that would keep him going for hours. The concupiscence I spelt out on those lines, though in reality I couldn't stand such, was enough to make a nun blush.

It was delicious torture receiving his replies, reading every word that revealed he, too, shared the same fantasies. His descriptions were wicked, like melting chocolates. I read his words until the paper was worn and the words barely legible. Then I settled back in my bed, a grin spread across my face, while my imaginations ran like wild fire on a harmattan forest.

Each time I reread his replies, I cracked a laugh, and it took a while to quit my giggles. The poor dude truly believed my nonsensical wishes, when we might never meet.

It just was not possible. I could never live up to the behaviour I confessed in those letters. The thought made my cheeks flame up. I clutched my reading table with sweaty palms. As though to hide my embarrassment, the curtains fluttered and settled over my face.

Mike was not in a hurry to meet me either. He promised, just as I requested, to take me to the middle of nowhere and bang all ounce of sense out of me—a promise I kept safe in the recess of my wanton heart.

Time flew, for almost two years, neither of us acted on our whorish thoughts.

—

I graduated from college, and Mike's business expanded internationally.

At thirty-one-years-old, he already owned several exportation companies that granted him leverage to mix with the elites. His rapid success attracted to him international friends.

His new societal status had me thinking he was not into me, that he was way out of my league, too big a fry. But he proved me wrong in his last letter that arrived in the second month of the year. February is my favourite month, our birth month. Mike and I were born the same month and day, 20th February.

He wrote to me about sneaking away from the city hustle to lie low. Every 20th February, he went to this hideout with a few friends to have wild fun. We had stayed away from each other for too long. My mind was made up on meeting him this year on our birthday. I would go with him to this hideout, and make it extra special for us.

"Can it be only you and I?" Mike requested. "Just the two of us, alone, isolated from the world. I want to be the only one who hears your screams when I drill your screws loose."

'Oh yes!' I replied, and then frowned. I doubted I was as sexy as I portrayed in those letters. Besides, if he believed I would go all the way and screw his brain out, just like I bragged, it was best not to go.

Still, I could not continue to hide. Soon enough, he would figure me out for who I am; a braggart, a snail who did nothing but tease and hide. To be honest, I wanted to experience all he wrote on those pages.

"I must be outta my mind," I screamed into the empty kitchen.

In the silence with the utensils for company and my chest heaving, realization dawned on me that, I had not only lost my mind but I was insane.

CHAPTER 2

My heart had not stopped its *thump thump* since I made up my mind to hook up with Mike on that trip. I had in my head a list of what I packed away in my small overnight suitcase; my sexiest undies, a few seductress' night wears, oversized t-shirts, flip-flops, my hand-mirror and make-up kit.

Only a day or two, nothing more, I reminded myself for the umpteenth time, a firm set to my chin. The more I repeated the reminder, the more my doubts increased. I didn't trust myself. I had no idea how far I was willing to go. If Mike insisted we stayed a bit longer, I wasn't sure if I would be able to say no or resist his charm.

I paced around the sitting room of my one bedroom apartment.

"You are a smart young lady," I muttered, clenching and unclenching my fingers. "Play the game, break the rules. Twist him around your little finger and get him to agree to your every whim."

Mike's car was already parked in front of my apartment at 3:00p.m. The pom pom of his horn, not only announced his presence, but his eagerness to get the party started. I grabbed my little suitcase off the dresser table and dashed out of the house. I stopped to lock my door before heading for his car.

Those magical butterflies danced in my stomach. This was our second meet since that day at The Church Of Angels two years ago. My knees jerked as I wondered whether I was better looking now than the girl he remembered from back then.

His eyes lit up as they followed my approach. That was a good sign, and my shoulders relaxed as he stepped out smartly to open the passenger's side of the car.

His smile broadened, just before he leaned in and whispered in my ears, "You are beautiful."

I looked up and smiled into his eyes.

"That should be a Tomford Sensational lady perfume you are wearing." His breathe smelt of fresh mint.

My eyes rested on his lips, deliciously tempting, inviting a kiss. His mouth brushed my cheeks lightly as he checked my seatbelt. He pulled away, tossed my bag into the backseat and went around the car. The tingling sensation from that brief contact grew as he slid into his seat.

He plugged in his seatbelt, started the car, then in a subtle but bold voice he asked, "Are you ready for an adventure?"

That was the perfect time to say no, an opportunity to back-out. I should tell him it was all a mistake and I have changed my mind. Instead, I nodded, ran my hands through my hair, and squared my shoulders, confident enough to ride any storm he'd throw my way.

His eyes ran over my face. Satisfied with what he saw, he squeezed my left hand and pulled away from the curb. We drove towards the city in company of the soft romantic blues from the car stereo.

"Where exactly are we going?" I asked at last, my curiosity getting the best of me. I didn't like the slight tremor in my voice. "I mean, we have been driving for hours." I sounded almost apologetic, as though my question needed this explanation.

He took his eyes off the road and flashed his teeth in a grin. "I told you it is a secret hideout, didn't I?"

"Sure, you did. I would love to go there, but the journey seems endless."

"Relax, Bliss." He used a fond pet-name, same one he called me in those letters. "Don't ruin the moment with questions. Secrecy makes the experience triple better. Trust me, will you?" His tone softened.

Maybe it was the tension of what lay ahead, or not knowing if I would go through with it. I couldn't stay clam as he requested.

"How far still?"

"Oh, dear." He gave me a look of chastisement, one he would use on a naughty child who tested his patience. Then he said in a condescending voice. "Are you hungry or famished?"

I shrugged and bit my lip, eyes on my fingers, ashamed of my behaviour.

He sighed. "We could stop and eat something," he offered and waited. When I said nothing, he continued, "I know a place that cooks something decent. The only snag is I asked my cooks at our secret spot to make a banquet, a buffet or whatever folks want to call it. For just the two of us."

He looked at me from the side of his eye. "But if you are this hungry, I won't mind stopping so you could grab a bite."

"No, thanks. I am not that hungry." I closed my eyes. "I am just tired and will love to rest"

"We will get there soon, dear. Now be a good sport and have some bliss from your name blissful," he kidded.

I laughed, and the sound loosened me up.

I must have slept off, because when I opened my eyes and checked my watch, several hours had passed. We were driving through the middle of nowhere. The car sped along a rocky pathway, and a right turn took us past a high gate that slid open on its own. I sat forward, unable to recognize the path ahead, I swerved around and looked at Mike. Whether he sensed my stare, he showed no sign. He kept his eyes glued on the windscreen, his feet stuck on the gas pedal.

I did not want to ask anymore questions or display childish fears. I turned around to gaze through my window. I could make out that we were in a compound with a long stretch of grassland and thick oak woods. The trees cleared to reveal a square-like structure whose architecture went back to the ancient Egyptians buildings and was covered with climbing shrubs. The house did not look like it housed more than two rooms.

I exhaled, finally we were here. Instead of this thought to comfort me, an uneasy feeling brewed.

"It is an old structure of my father," Mike offered an explanation without my prompting. "I refurnished the interior but left the exterior as it were. Leaving it this way makes the place mysterious. All my friends who visited have got the same look you have now." He chuckled. "It is priceless, especially when they see the interior."

He stopped the car and jumped out. He came around to my side of the door before I could open it. I smiled my thanks, and let him hold my hand.

He led me along a long pathway of marbles and inside the house.

The interior was a splash of cozy, modern decor just as he did described it. The fireplace was designed with rubies and every item glinted gold or sapphire. I smiled, now certain I didn't need much convincing to stay longer than a day or two. I followed behind him. From what I gleaned in the fast walk along a narrow corridor, the house was an underground building with about three rooms. He stopped in front of a door which he announced would serve as my room for the duration of my visit.

"Have a warm bath, change up and come upstairs for dinner." He had that smile which, though seductive, was a bit unsettling. "I can volunteer to bath you, if you won't mind, Bliss." He winked, amusement played around his lips.

I swallowed and averted my eyes. "No, no, thanks, Mike." I blabbed, winced, and then cleared my throat. "I am sure you are tired from all that driving. Maybe you could do that for me tomorrow, if the offer is still up then."

"Do what tomorrow?" he prompted, a trace of laughter lingered in his voice.

My head jerked up and I caught the merry twinkle in his eyes. I raised my chin and met his gaze. "Scrub me down, you know."

"All right, it is a deal." He reached over to tuck a loose strand of hair behind my ear, paused to sniff my fragrance.

With a slow searching look at my face, he turned around and went back the way he came without a backward glance.

Dinner was a quiet affair.

We concentrated on the meal and did little to no talking. I did not see the servers. The meals were all laid out on the table by the time I found the dinning room.

After dinner, I opted to see a movie. Mike chose one from the lot which he promised was a romantic movie, but turned out to be a steamy soft porn. He relaxed into the couch beside me with a soft chuckle that came out more like a dare for me to walk out.

I couldn't chicken out on a mere movie, so I sat tight and prayed the romp session on the screen would not get any more heated than it was. His hand reached across my back and squeezed my shoulder as if in approval, like I just passed a test. I looked up at his face and saw him watching me. He ran his tongue over his lips, and when I opened my mouth to speak, his head swooped down and engulfed me in a kiss.

I hesitated but gave in, granting his tongue entrance. He found my tongue and we both played in each other's mouth. He licked the roof of my mouth, sending a tingling sensation down my spin, warm fluid slid down my thighs. This was heaven, a thousand times better than I imagined. He gently unbuttoned my shirt enough to expose my hard nipples.

Then he kissed my neck, trailed up to my ear, showering pecks like soft roses around my earlobe. He moaned as his tongue wrapped around my exposed nipple, made taunt by the slight evening chill. I shuddered, unable to control the thrill that ran through me.

The pleasure was unbearable. That spot, gosh!

His head went to my belly button, sending shock volts through me. I shivered, feeling the rush of a powerful volcano. No one had ever touched me that way; in fact, my belly button had never been touched. A burning sensation erupted when he buried his head under my skirt and licked my clit.

"Say my name," he commanded, his tongue darting around the patch between my legs.

I caught my breath. "M-m-ike," I stammered, trembling like a rain-soaked leaf.

He pulled up his head, releasing me from my torture. He turned me around.

"Bend over," he whispered, "and don't look."

I struggled with the words. "M-m-mike, let us continue a little longer." My tongue flickered over my upper lip. "I love it."

"Don't look," he croaked, "just bend over, Bliss."

I struggled to turn around, in need of more smooching, but he held down my shoulder and gently bent me over.

"Bliss, don't!"

But I saw it. Mike's hands were of more volume than was humanly possible. But it was his face that stopped me. His eyes shone red and bright, pupils glowed scarlet, and when I looked down, a tail dangled, swiping behind him.

"What have you become, Mike?" I let out a squeal, and my scream filled the chamber.

CHAPTER 3

"What have you become, Mike?" I wailed and closed my eyes. I crossed myself. "Blood of the living Jesus Christ!"

I felt silly inviting God into such atmosphere, knowing what was about to go down a while ago. But I was out of option for help. God seemed my best bet at that moment. Although, I wasn't into religion, I grew up in a Christian family. My shoulders slumped in guilt.

Mike's bloody eyes glowed in the dim light of the sitting room. He bared his teeth in a snarl and pranced away.

I ran so fast I couldn't feel my legs. I flung the door open and raced down the path as though I flew. Panting and out of breath, the gate zoomed into view a little distance ahead. I increased my pace until I was close enough to attempt a leap, a futile attempt to scale the high gate over to the other side. The gate was way high and too smooth for me to grasp and climb.

Tears of frustration ran down my cheeks. Going back into that house was out of the question. I slumped to the ground and drew my knees to my chin, legs tucked close to my stomach.

I stared at the structure behind. Mike wasn't coming after me. He allowed me to have my moment until pitch dark came.

I saw the feet in front of me, before I heard him speak.

"Bliss, please, let us go inside."

The voice startled me. I squeaked and crawled back on my bum and hands, determined to put as much distance as I could between us. He stepped forward.

"Come in with me. Give me a chance to explain what you just saw in there." In the dark, he held out something that looked like my shirt.

"Get away from me, you beast," I snarled. "I rebuke you in the name of my Lord Jesus."

Mike laughed, a soft mocking sound. "I am rebuked, Bliss, but please, be sensible enough to come inside and get to bed."

The tears flowed faster. I had no clue what I signed up for, what I had gotten my self into. I wasn't sure I would survive the night. I could see my death almost happening.

"Get away from me, you demon," I cursed, hoping my voice had enough bark to let him know I was not afraid of him.

Mike settled on the grass patch, a little distance from me.

"Bliss, I am different. I knew this when I was barely eighteen-years-old." He buried his face in his hands, rocking his upper torso. When the hands dropped away, his voice was steadier. "I have hurt no one, Bliss."

"I don't know what the hell you are saying." I tried to control the panic in my voice. I was a step away from hysterical.

"I will not hurt you." A strangled gasp escaped him. "I have my transformation under control. It only happens when I am in love with a lady or excited like I was with you in there."

"I do not want to hear anymore." Tears made my voice shake.

"Sorry, I cannot let you out this night. You will get hurt out there on the lonely road. It is unbelievable, one minute you have the hots for me, and the next, you are looking at me as if I am the devil."

I said nothing, hoping he would get bored, leave me and go away but it did not happen.

"I have not loved a girl or fallen in love. I had my fair share of fun and sex without any emotions attached. That is why I have not transformed for a long while and my secret remained safe. You came along, Bliss, and tonight I got extremely turned on. Bliss, I love—"

I cut him short. "Oh, spare me all that crap, will you? Prince of darkness, you think I am an easy target to initiate?" I spat the words at him. "Mike! Open the gate or this will become a kidnap."

His tone remained calm. "I do not expect you to stay or accept me. Tomorrow, I will drive you home. If you will forgive me and listen, then I will tell you how I got to be like this during the ride."

Though what he said about endangering myself this late at night rang true, I did not want to return to that eerie structure.

"I asked the cook to bake you a cake. It should be ready to cut now. Forgive me, Bliss, I ruined our birthday." He rose. "I will just go in, disappear to my room, and you can stay in yours until morning."

He shuffled his feet, waiting for me to rise. I remained seated.

"Goodnight, Bliss." He walked off, head bowed.

My eyes followed the outline of his figure. A little distance away, he turned back to stare at the spot where I sat as though a thought just occurred to him.

"I will leave the gate keys on the dinning table. It is a tiny remote control. To unlock, press the green button but, please, the distance to the main road is too far and the route quite confusing for you to attempt alone."

I prayed for a miracle to teleport me to my house. I murmured the Lords prayer, and wondered if my earlier sluttish intention hindered my outrageous request.

I counted to fifty, enough time for him to get back into the house and lock himself somewhere out of my way. Then I stood and walked down the path he took. It was quiet inside the house. I saw the gate key on the long table across the dinning hall, just like he promised. I sniffed in the aroma of freshly baked chocolate cake that filled the hall, tip-toed to the table, pressed the green button and ran out as fast as my leg could carry.

I tried to put on my shirt without slowing my pace. At the T-junction on the rocky path, I paused to catch my breath, and buttoned up my shirt. The silence in the street was jarring. Not a soul was in sight on the dark lane.

Figuring which of the roads to take was next to impossible. I guess if God wasn't angry with me, he might send a car cruising with a driver willing to help. The thought had barely formed, when I saw pair of headlights in the distance.

"Oh, thank you big guy in the sky." My relief was so great, I almost wept, breathing hard as I walked, half-ran to the middle of the road.

I waved wildly, hoping the car's lights would pick me out in the dark, before the driver rode close enough to slam into me. A few feet from me, the car slowed. I watched the driver's window wound.

An anxious, baritone voice enquired, "What are you doing out here alone at this time of the night, lady?"

I didn't blame him. I guess I looked a bit out of my mind, or worse I could be a ghost on the prowl.

I covered the short distance, and made out a bit of his features. "It is a long story, sir, but please, can you drop me off at the highway?'

"Get in," he ordered and leaned across his seat to open the passenger's door.

I went around the car, jumped in and slammed the door. My heart beat hard against my chest as I heard the automatic lock snap into place.

"Seat belt, please," he said.

I drew the belt across my breasts. "Thank you, sir. My name is Bliss..ful."

He smiled and put the car into gear. "I know."

My head snapped around, I gaped. The voice.

"Have we met before?"

"I believe so. The name is Mike."

"M-m-ike?" A scream rose to my throat at the coincidence. Same voice, but there was no way this man could be Mike. He looked nothing like him. Unless one of his powers was to transform into another individual.

"Stop."

He raised an eyebrow. "Pardon?"

"Stop the car!" I screamed. I pulled the door handle, but the security lock jammed it in place. I turned around to snatch the steering wheel.

It was him. The same Mike I ran away from.

My head swam, darkness rose and I passed out.

CHAPTER 4

A different ceiling hung up there. This was not my room. I let my neck roll to the side, taking in the unfamiliar, similar to my foster brother's house in Texas. Maybe that was where I am at the moment. Everything appeared well arranged. A neat person must live here, I thought as my sight blurred. Through the film that glazed my eyes, I caught a glimpse of sometime colourful.

"Balloons and roses," I mumbled. "Today must be someone's birthday."

Then it clicked.

Birthday! I jumped off the luxury bed, and came up short as I saw Mike at one corner of the room, the size of my living room back home.

"Jesus Christ!" Memory trickled. "Mike, we were about going off for a jolly ride when I slept off." I frowned, my eyes not leaving his face. "But something scared me off. What was it?"

Mike walked towards me, his face lined with confusion. I could see he did not sleep well.

"It must be the rocky road. Remember we were going on a jolly-ride as you said, and you slept off. I brought us back home to sleep." He winked.

I massage my temple. "I feel awkward, like something more happened. Something . . . bad."

He scoffed. "Don't be silly."

"I mean it, Mike. My spirit speaks when I am troubled, or about to get into trouble, or confused like this."

He crossed his arms over his chest, contemplating whether to take me seriously or laugh.

"Mike, the Holy Spirit is trying to minister to me," I insisted, not about to be put off by his disbelieving expression.

"We might use this ministration to win a lottery."

"I mean it!" I glared and stomp my feet.

He raised his hands in a truce. "Okay. Tell me about this Spirit who is Holy." He cocked his head. "My late paternal grandmother had the same intuition thing. My father told me about it. He said it worked much for her, that she was special, like you." He snapped his fingers, a mischievous grin spreading. "Perhaps, this intuition phenomenon is a woman thing that we, men, are immune to."

"Perhaps." I rolled my eyes.

He came closer and touched my check. "How do you like my room?"

I turn to give it a sweeping glance. "I love it, masculine but cozy, just like the living area." I fanned his ego. "Mind showing me to the rest of the house?"

"Sure, I'll be honoured, my lady." He curved his elbow for me to pass my hand through the loop, and led me into each room.

"Lovely," I echoed.

The tour ended at the kitchen with me meeting and greeting some of his workers. Everyone beamed and said a hello, except Mrs. Elena. He introduced her as his head chef, she had served his late father.

"She's part of the family and I deeply respect her," he emphasized.

"Nice to meet you," I said to the stone-faced woman.

"An absolute pleasure." The lie in her comeback rolled off as thick as a rock.

We passed the laundry room and entered the gym area.

"Can we sit here a bit and talk about your intuition?" Mike made funny faces.

"Fine! Sit over there, mister." I pointed at one of the gym equipment.

"Yes, teacher." He settled into the equipment and looked with an expectant expression.

"Let me brief you about the Holy Spirit." I cleared my throat. "Anytime I am about to get into danger, I hear whispers."

He frowned. "Whispers?"

I nodded and tapped my chest. "Right here, in my mind. The whisper tells me the kind of danger ahead and how to avoid it."

"Interesting." He crossed his legs. "Strange but interesting."

"She is the comforter, sent to help me win." I giggled.

"Wow!"

I raised my hand. "Be quiet. You might hear her."

"I think I hear her," Mike whispered. "She said I should kiss you."

We burst into laughter.

I choked and fell towards the aerobics mat, but he caught my arm. I fell against him instead.

"Bliss, I am falling in love with you. From the first day we met, I sensed something strong and powerful about you." He smiled in that mischievous way. "But I never knew it was called intuition or the Holy Spirit."

I stared at Mike, handsome, gentle, bold, rich, young and well-mannered. Who would not want him?

"But I am not ready for a relationship." It was time for me to come clean. "All those letters was not the real me. I am not sexually strong." I forced myself to meet his gaze. "I meant none of it."

Mike threw back his head and laughed. "Bliss, relax. It is not about sex. I do not want us to go into that till we are maybe engaged or married."

I did not believe a young man with such looks and body could stick to a no sex relationship or even succumb to a non sexual relationship.

He cut me in my thoughts. "I still have erections, if that is what you are wondering about."

I hid my embarrassment behind a cough.

"Bliss, be my lady, please."

"I agree on the no sex relationship," I wagged a finger, "but you are on probation until I figure out why my spirit is troubled."

"Yes, my lady," he said in his most serious voice. "Thank you so much, sweetie. You are truly blissful, my Bliss."

He held my hand and we strolled into the garden. He talked about nature and his love for it. That night, we cuddled and he repeated how lucky he was to have me.

Mornings were heaven. Mike woke me with a kiss, breakfast and roses. He wanted us to stay a week or two, and I was fine with it.

After all, I just graduated from school and he had people managing his business. So we were both fine. Until . . . .

CHAPTER 5

Until I eavesdropped a conversation between him and Mrs. Elena outside his bedroom door.

"How is she doing now?" I heard Mrs. Elena say.

"Asleep, I just left her in bed." It was Mike's voice.

"I mean, how is she acting? Does she remember your transformation?"

"She is perfectly normal, she has no clue."

"Good. I told you to let me handle that. It is up to you to play well and win," a brief pause, "if you want her as wife like you told me earlier."

"Yes."

"Be careful not to involve a lot of passion or affection in this. I know you love her deeply, but be wise, son. You remember how your father died?"

"He had a heart attack that killed him."

"Don't be foolish, son. You were only six-years-old at the time, but I and your grandmother have told you the truth. A heart attack was a cover up for the press and the public, not for you."

"Yes."

"Your father had a great love for your mother, just as you do for this one."

"But—"

"But he didn't know how to control his affection. Most times he transformed before her and I always stepped in to wipe it off her memory, son. Our tribe queried your father on this many times. He was almost summoned by the Highest Angel Of The Church for revealing himself unduly to humans. Our law states that family is only same blood. Your mum was his wife, but she was not family. Too much affection for your mother ended badly. She killed him, Mike."

"I don't believe my mother is capable of murder." There is a strain in the voice. "Aunt Elena, I have had this conversation with mum several times. She insists dad's family lied to implicate her, and I believe her."

"You are young and capable of believing anything. Your mother had the same intuition as what you told me about Bliss. I bet your good mother didn't tell you that she worships a higher God, the Holy Spirit. Am I right, son?"

"We are the highest species."

"Of course, but only in our hierarchy. When last did you and your mother speak to each other?"

A hesitation. "Almost ten years now."

"Find her son, and tell her about the woman you are in love with, alongside that intuition thing. She might have the best advice for you."

The conversation stopped. I heard footsteps approaching the door, and I jumped back into bed and stretched my arms over my head, pretending I just woke up.

"Eh, my pretty lady," Mike teased from the door. "Look who just snapped out from a beauty sleep."

I smiled, hoping nothing on my face gave away my horror from the conversation I just overheard.

"Launch or movies?" Mike raised an eyebrow.

I needed an excuse to go back home. I jumped off the bed, and threw on my shirt. "Mike, I don't like it here. All we do is eat, sleep and see a movie. No fun, not even sex." I breathed fast at the end of my rant.

I mentioned sex since Mike was not down with that. He avoided sex with me in order not to 'transform', whatever transforming meant. He might have a temper, a huge sexual appetite, or he could be a molester. Why did his mother kill his Father who loved her deeply? If I get him to have sex with me, I could see what he was hiding.

"Make love to me, Mike." I walked up to stand before him.

"C'mon, Bliss. We agreed on no sex relationship, remember?" He shook his head as if I had gone crazy, and walked out of the room.

I followed him down the stairs. "I don't remember such agreement. No sex? Why am I here with you? Why are we together? Answer me. Stop there, Mike," I yelled.

He hesitated at the dinning table, pulled out one of the chairs, and sank into it.

"What has come over you? Stop trying to be who you are not, Bliss."

"I want you, Mike."

He held my wrists. "Pull yourself together, please. I am doing this because I love you."

"This is how you treat someone you love?" I pulled off my shirt, shook myself out of my innerwear, and sat on the table. His eyes bulged.

"W-what are you doing?" Mike croaked.

I parted my legs, dipped my ring finger inside my hole and tweaked my clit. I beckoned him over with my pinky finger.

"Come over here, Mike. Come inside me, honey," I purred. "Make me feel like a woman, like someone you love. Let's cum together. Don't keep your lady waiting."

"Bliss, please." His voice sounded strangled.

"Is your dick working or not, Mike?"

He rose and came to me.

I lifted my legs to his broad shoulders. Our eyes meet as he parted my clit with his thumb and forefinger, lowered his tongue and sucked. I screamed from pleasure, shame, and then fear, a thousand thoughts ran through my head.

"Mikeeee," I moaned.

I dripped as he dipped his middle finger into his mouth and pushed it inside me, at first slow, soon it became rhythmic strokes.

"Stop, Mike!" My voice shook.

He licked my belly buttons. His weight pressed against me as his lips found mine, and then moved on to bite my earlobe, like a happy puppy at the sight of its owner.

My eyes darted to the cutleries at the centre of the table. I grabbed a table knife, and slipped it under my hair. That was my backup plan *if* he transformed. I moaned when his tongue struck the g-spot. Busy down there, he failed to notice my move.

On a mission to ravish every piece of me, he held my hands above my head and latched his lips around my nipple, almost swallowing a whole breast. He gave the twin molds playful love bites that sent waves of sweet pains over my body.

He was wild but it felt good, if only I could ignore this annoying fear. Raising his waist, his huge dick pushed into me.

I winced at the unfamiliar pain and bit my lip, determined not to let him notice I was hurting. I wanted this moment. He slammed into me, hitting hard and fast. An eerie sound filled the room as he expelled, his hardness ramming into me.

Between pleasure and fear, I struggled to speak. "Mike, please, stop."

"Why?" he gasped, not losing tempo.

"Don't cum inside me, please. I am ovulating."

"Remember? We will cum together and stay in it to dry?" He repeated the words I had written to him. "We will climb the peak together, honey."

He rammed with such force that I let out a moan of delicious pleasure.

His deep baritone voice rasped in my ear. "Sweetie, I am Cumming." He thrust faster, jerked and his back stiffened, his seed releasing inside me.

He collapsed on top of me. Our heart matched pace until he rose, kissed my forehead, and ascended the stairs to his room.

I laid there on the table and covered my face with my palms. He did not transform. I rolled over on my side and sat up, aware of the tears that slid down my cheeks. He left me here, used. I retrieved the knife, climbed off the table and stomped upstairs to his room. I turned the knob but the door did not budge. I put my ear to the wood panel and made out cricket chirpings and the hiss of a scorpion. I jerked back as if stung, my legs soft under me like jelly. I leaned on the threshold, and a few seconds passed as I tried to steady myself. Then I peeped through the keyhole.

Hunched in the barely lit room, a huge shadow-like creature knelt. It possessed the form of a man-scorpion creature, from the trembling of its shoulders, it seemed to be weeping.

I banged a fist on the door. "Mike, open up! I know you are in there."

The knob turned and the door open half-way.

I pushed it in the rest of the way and entered. He stood naked, unmoving. And when I got close, I noticed the tears that stained his cheeks..

"I love you, Bliss." He pulled me to himself and clutched me in a hug, then his grip relaxed. "What is this?" He held up my hand which gripped the table knife as if it was a dagger.

CHAPTER 6

"The weird sound from your room got me anxious. I grabbed the nearest weapon I could lay my hands on, and came to save you."

"You really came to save me?" he asked in an incredulous voice.

I nodded, and tried to look solemn.

"Oh dear, Bliss, that was so brave of you." Confusion darted across his face. "But I didn't hear any sound. I locked the door in order to use the toilet."

I stepped back. "Oh, my bad then." I turned and fled.

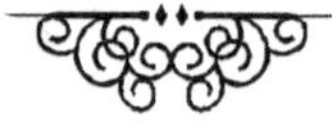

We stayed apart since that mind-blowing sex. I went out of my way to avoid Mike, kept to the kitchen in an attempt to get close to Mrs. Elena. Her stiff façade remained impenetrable, as she maintained an official front with me. I avoided sleeping in Mike's room, a move that did not go down well with him.

Knock, knock. A knuckle rapped.

"Who is it?"

"May I come in?" Mike's voice came from the other side of my door.

"Of course."

He entered and shut the door soundlessly. I watched him walk up and sat on my bed.

He leaned forward. "Sweetie, why are you avoiding me?"

I opened my mouth to protest.

He continued, "You spend a lot more time with Aunt Elena. Highly commendable, but twenty-four hours in the kitchen is absurd. We came to relax, and that is what you should be doing."

"I am bored, Mike. What else can I do here?"

"There's the Gym, library, and don't forget the Jacuzzi." He ticked them off his fingers. "You can utilize these facilities, Bliss."

I hesitated. "I will check out the library"

"You mentioned a love for romance novels. We have a number of them lying around on the shelves." He slapped my backside. "Meanwhile, your birthday gift get here in a week," he called over his shoulder, exiting the living room.

Alone again. Being on my own seemed a recurring pattern. I went off in search of the library and found it after a few wrong turns. I slipped in, went through the titles on the shelves, pulled a few out and placed them on the reading table.

Done with scouting, I flopped into one of the chairs to read but one of the titles caught my eyes. I pulled it out to confront a cover picture of a dark creature with multiple hands and a long tail. The title read, *The Transforming Angels*.

"Might make for an interesting read," I muttered, ran my palm over the front, and coughed as the rising dust choked me.

I flipped through the pages until I spotted a chapter on '*How To Kill The Soul Of A Transforming Angel*'. I scanned through the chapter, and was soon engrossed.

Midnight crept on, carried away on killing the soul of transforming creatures, in this case, Mike.

"Bliss." Mike's steps approached the library.

I put the book away, shuffled it amidst the pile on the table.

"I am in the Library," I yelled.

His hip leaned against the door frame, a smile puckering his lips.

"Missed me?" I chuckled. "I hope not too much."

"I cannot sleep alone tonight after what we experienced earlier." He held his palm up as though swearing to the national flag. "Sleep in my room tonight. I promise to be good." His grin promised the opposite.

I wasn't convinced one bit. "I can't imagine you as good. I like your naughty self, Mike."

He drew me close, eyes laughing and lifted me in his arms.

"Shall we?" He marched upstairs with me nestled in his arms, my hands wrapped around his neck.

I only released him as he lowered me into the bed and served me dinner. I took a warm shower later, and we cuddled all night. It took all I had not act odd. Going around my head were ways to gather the items needed to experiment the potions described in the book. I needed one potent enough to slay the souls of transformed angels. For the duration it would take me to put things in place, I must act overly nice around Mike, and entrap him into an emotional state that would surge his transformation. Only then could I kill his soul and set him free.

The next day, after breakfast, I set the wheel in motion. My experience as a biochemist aided in figuring out the household item that contained poisonous chemical substances. I went for an empty glass jar from the kitchen cupboard, lifted several batteries from the Ac remote, toothpaste tubes, and match boxes. In the library, a portion of the table became an emergency laboratory.

My urine, peed inside a jar, contained the bicarbonate ions I needed. I dismantled the dry cell batteries to extract the dark ash, a host for manganese dioxide. I added the ashes from the match sticks, and squeezed in the toothpaste. It gave me the needed sodium Lauryl sulphate, toxic enough to ignite irritation or cancers. Almost done, I poured in a little whisky I snatched from the bar to tie the elements together. The rising foam was the exact result I hoped for, toxic enough to kill a transforming demon. I hid the jar behind the book shelves and hopped a little dance, humming to my favourite song.

Footsteps echoed as they neared the library. I rid the table of tell-tale signs, made the remnant of my specimens disappear as I hid them in corners. I hurried back to my seat, picked up a romance novel and pretended to read.

Mrs. Elena opened the door, her usual official self.

"Hello, Bliss."

"Hello, Mrs. Elena."

She grunted. "Mike is alone and looking lost. I asked about you, got told you locked yourself in here all day." She entered the room to survey my table, her hands behind her back like a teacher. "I see you are engulfed in your reading. I used to be that engrossed, too. But that was when we lost Mike's father and I tried to read away my sorrow."

She paused, as though waiting for me to say something. I had nothing to say, so I waited.

"I came to speak with you on something important, Bliss."

She was so close to the table, I tilted my head back to stare at her.

"Do not hesitate to speak to me about anything at all, whenever you feel like talking to someone. Is that alright with you?" She had a half- smile.

"Sure, thanks." I rose, making her to step back. "I was on my way to meet up with Mike. I am sure he misses my presence."

Without waiting for her response, I turned towards the shelf and shoved the novel back in its place. Then I walked past her and out.

"Good idea," she gushed and shut the library door, following me out of the room.

I found Mike tucked in one of the sofas in the living room. He held a glass of liquor, his eyes fixed on a movie.

I walked up behind him and wrapped my arms around his broad shoulders, caressing his neck. I slipped my fingers into his shirt, my palm ran over his hairy chest and paused around his nipples.

"I know you missed me, honey," I whispered.

He looked at me from over his shoulder, smiled, and passed me the glass he was nursing.

"Take a sip, Bliss. I held myself in check with this. I am going insane thinking about you, baby."

I chuckled. "I need you sane and happy."

I came around the sofa, slid on his laps, and stole a kiss.

"Wow, you are really excited today, love. What book blew your mind this way?"

I laughed.

"Let me guess."

I panicked he might mention *The Book Of The Angels* so I interrupted. "It is a *Kiss of A Deadly Rose* by Katrina Adams. Powerful storyline."

"Yep, powerful," he agreed. "I see you like romance and horror genre. That book has a dark story in between the chapters. Did you read up to chapter nine?".

"I only got up to chapter four before I came searching for you. I am enjoying the romantic twist.

"What is for launch?" I changed topic.

"Aunt Elena is making us chicken soup. A favourite of mine."

"Is it okay to do alcohols tonight?

"Let's just have fun, Bliss."

"I will love to get a little tipsy tonight. We can do karaoke with our tipsy voices."

"Let the fun begin." He lifted me and spun me around,

CHAPTER 7

A car horn blasted, jerking Mike awake. He picked up the remote and pressed the green button programmed to slide the gate open.

"Come here, Bliss," he said. His smile remained as I walked into his open arms. "Your birthday gift is here."

I wrapped my hands around him, raised my face and pecked his cheek. "Let us go see it, darling."

Holding hands, we went down the stairs and into the garage. The latest BMW i8 coupe in my favourite colour, red, parked in the centre of the space.

A huge man in suit strolled towards us.

"A happy birthday to you both." He beamed, a bunch of keys dangling from outstretched hand. He passed Mike some documents and produced a pen with a flourish. "Sign here."

Mike read the lines before passing the papers to me. "Happy birthday, my lady. Please, put your signature right here."

His eyes smiled at mine. Assured, I signed the dotted lines and kissed him.

"Pete, thanks a lot." Mike gave the man a firm handshake. "I will see you in town."

"I appreciate," Pete said and walked out of the garage and down the path that led to the gate.

Mike turned to me. "Do you love your car?"

"Oh yes! Especially that it came in red. Can we go on a test ride?"

"Evening will be a perfect time to drive out of town and back."

The time was fine, but I wasn't sure what to do once we got to town. Running away might be a good move. Inside the house, I hurried to the syringe pack in the First Aid Box shelve, took one out and carried on to the library for the chemical concoction.

"Mike." Mrs. Elena's voice edged close to the library.

I slid to the living room, syringe hidden under my shirt.

"Yes, Aunt," Mike said. "I am in the gym."

"Okay, I am coming over there," she said.

I tiptoed and hid behind the hallway door with enough room for me to spy on them without giving myself away.

"Mike, I wondered what Bliss is up to, spending that much time in the library. So I decided take a look."

"Of course, she is reading *Kiss Of A Deadly Ross*. You have read that book, right?"

"And what else?"

"Nothing. Just reading. Why?"

"Hmmm, I found some concoction behind the book shelve and smelt it. Seems like she planned to poison you.

"Bliss studied biochemistry. She might have decided to experiment, and then kept it safe behind the book shelve, you know."

"All right, Mike. Believe whatever you want, but I wonder why she kept that experiment away from you."

"Relax, aunty. I trust her. She and most humans are incapable of killing us. They might want to, but lack the guts. Most of them with the Holy Spirit lack knowledge of its powers, neither do they believe in themselves. I have related with them for years, and I know what I am saying."

"If you insist. Do not say I did not warn you." Mrs. Elena's steps made no sound as she moved away.

I tiptoed after her and kept a discreet distance in the shadows. She paused at the kitchen door and exhaled.

"Confident like his father," she muttered. "Humans have no guts to kill us." She pushed the door open and entered the kitchen.

I ran back to the library, grabbed the rest concoction, and emptied it inside my room's toilet bowl. With no idea how to discard the syringe, I shoved it in the pocket of Mike's shorts which I wore.

CHAPTER 8

"A wonderful dinner, Mike. Thank you." I had not eaten a more delicious chicken soup.

Mike nodded and flashed sparkling white teeth. "Can we test drive the car now?" A boyish eagerness laced his tone.

"I am ready." I twirled like a ballerina.

"I love this side of you." He reached for my hand, and we walked out the path that led to the garage for my car.

"Where are you love-birds heading?" Mrs. Elena stepped out from the shadows.

"Test driving. We might not return tonight." Mike's laughter rang with meanings.

"Okay." She faded as quietly as she had come.

Mike held the driver's door and ushered me in. He settled into the passenger's seat, strapped on his belt and said, "Ready?"

He pressed the little remote to open the gate.

I started the car. "Which way, Mike?"

"Take a right, through the rocky path. I will handle the wheel when you are tired. Hell, we might lodge out and return tomorrow, sweetie."

I drove slowly through the rocky path, nodding to the classical tune from the stereo.

Mike spoke abruptly. "I never want to be without you." He touched my hand.

"I am driving, Mike."

"Pull over and let me drive instead."

I leveled the car by the rocky path, turned off the ignition, reached over and kissed him deep.

"I am falling for you, too." I said against his lips.

He pressed a little knob by the side of my seat, and it reclined all the way to the back like a bed. I dragged him over as our kiss intensified. I pressed my thighs together as a wetness formed between my legs. He released my mouth, his head lowered to bite my nipple through my shirt. I moaned and clutched his shoulder, trembling as he unbuttoned my shirt just enough to get to my nipples. His fingers tweaked them, then his tongue wrapped around my right boob.

"Make love to me, Mike."

I unzipped his trousers and wrapped my mouth around his huge erect dick. My hands stroked the length of his massive cock. I let my tongue work its ways on his scrotum, took his dick in my mouth, and when he moaned, his fingers dug into my hair.

"Bliss, honey, I love you so much."

He turned me around, so we were in a 69 position. He pulled down my short and gave my V area a good suck. I moaned, the pleasure unbearable, and dipped my forefinger inside his ass hole as his tongue reached my G-spot.

Then I saw the long tail spring up in my face.

"Jesus!"

"Relax, Bliss, I will not hurt you," the creature said. "Relax," it quipped in Mike's voice.

I yanked out the syringe, and shoved it into the thing that spoke like Mike, injecting its right leg.

He swatted at my hand. "Bliss, please. Don't do that."

I took out the syringe, the same time he slapped it out of my grip. He jerked the door handle, slammed his body against it and fell out. I leaned over the side, and instead of one, I saw two creatures with similar features. I pulled the door, but the second creature's tail slid in the partition and stopping it from closing completely.

"Don't hurt her, aunt Elena, please," the creature with Mike's voice screamed.

"Mrs. Elena?" I gasped.

That creature, undeniably Mrs. Elena, charged in a mad dash. It pinned my head against the car dash board, hot bestial breath fanning my face. Mike staggered from the effect of the concoction. He dragged the creature off me and wrestled it to the floor.

I groped for the car key, shaking and unable to think straight.

What did I do to Mike? Why is Mrs. Elena here?

I jumped out of the car, and hurried over to the other creature wrestling Mike, slashing with sharpencd claws and tearing him. I turned around to flee but heard Mike yelp in pain, and I stopped.

"Aunt Elena, why are you doing this?" Mike choked.

"I prepared to marry your father, but guess what? He married a human instead of me, chose your no-good mother over me," the creature roared. "All the promises he made, not one did he fulfill. He promised his son will marry my daughter, Ketany, but he sent you abroad instead. He had to die. I KILLED HIM! Now you want to marry this human? She, too, must die."

Mike slapped her with his tail, and both creatures tumbled to the ground, wrestling like wild demons. I stood, transfixed, watching Mike sag, his strength weakening at a steady pace. The injection got the better part of him.

I caught sight of the syringe on the ground with some concoction still in it and I dashed for it. With a yell, I jumped on the creature. She slapped me with her tail, released Mike and grabbed my throat as though to bite the side of my neck. Then she stopped.

"TABORA!" she screamed. "She is Tabora, not Bliss."

Mike groaned from the ground, his gaze fixed on us. "Tabora?" he growled, his befuddlement obvious.

"She is your sister, the one our community took from your mother at the age of three. She possessed both your mother's spirit and ours. She is powerful. I have to kill her now." Her teeth swooped to bite my head off.

Mike pushed to his feet, and grabbed her.

"Bliss, chant *Tabora hum om Bekanze Bekanze sirbu*, unlock your spirit and transport yourself home. She will kill you if you do not."

"No," I screamed at him, not believing their nonsense..

"She will kill you," Mike shouted, his strength waning. "Chant. Chant."

Mrs. Elena roared, her rage doubled. She jumped on Mike's back and her claw pierced his side. I gasped as he fell. The veil creature jumped on him to finish him off.

Sucking in my breath, my voice trembling, I chanted, certain I said them wrong. "*Tobara h-um om Bekan....ze em em em biritam bota*"

Everything went dark.

CHAPTER 9

I opened my eyes. Something cold pressed against my back. I lay naked atop an elevated, altar-like structure.

"A rebirth." A man's voice boomed from the side.

I turned my head to see the figure in a white robe. He stood statue-like and gave me a fixed stare.

"Welcome," he said after a while.

"Who are you?" I croaked. My voice felt parched and unused. I swallowed and tried again. "Where am I?" I wondered if my fear showed in my eyes.

A muscle twitched in his jaw. "I am Thompson, Emperor of the Angels in Canada province," he said in a toneless voice, and then spread his arms. "This is my secret altar. You were birthed today. But from your look the time you appeared, you chanted the wrong words and mistakenly teleported here. A proper rebirth should be in our headquarters' altar in the U.S.A."

"What will you do with me?" I felt groggy. The man, the place, everything seemed surreal.

He held out a red robe. "Wrap yourself, and sit over there." He pointed to a high-stool beside the altar. "You must relax, and tell me what happened."

I wrapped the robe around me, and let him assist me down the altar and to the stool he indicated.

"What do you want to know?"

"Ah," he snapped his fingers, "we can begin with who you are and how you got here."

I licked my dry lips, not sure if I could trust him enough to request for a glass of water. "I am Blissful. Mrs. Elena attacked me and killed my boyfriend." The tears spilled. I swiped it away angrily with the back of my palm.

"It is okay, dear." His voice had lost some of its lifelessness. "You may hold off telling me the story for now." He lifted my arm. "Let me look at you. With your birth being today, you must have an identification mark somewhere." He tipped my neck to the side.

"What are you doing?"

He laughed, and his eyes became friendlier. "You are Tabora, not Blissful. Hmmm, your father was a good friend and senior member of The Church of the Angels. They killed him and we—," he paused in respect of the memory, "a few of us in the community protected your mother. We helped her escape the vengeance of the elders and High Angel"

"Vengeance?"

"The Church accused her of killing your father."

"All you say doesn't make sense."

"Be patient. It will fall into place soon. Tabora, you were taken from your mother at age three, but we stole you from the headquarters, and returned you to your mother. After a while, she told us she adopted you out."

"Why will my mother give me away? Does she not want me?"

He shook his head. "Not at all. Quiet the opposite, really. She wanted to give you a new life. Your mother loved your father and her kids so much. The reason we stood by her against the community rulers is simple; your father would have wanted that for her. He would have done the same for us. So we owed him."

I looked at the man, afraid to interrupt this strange story.

"Thankfully, you landed here, Tabora, and not in the hands of the wrong angel. I will not go ahead with the rebirth process. It will remain as if you never chanted a rebirth code. Actually, you never did, because you got it all wrong and no ritual performed." He smiled, pleased with his own logic.

I had no idea what that meant for me, whether good or bad.

"We will get to find out truly if your brother is dead or still alive later. But right now, I will notify your mother. She has to come over as quickly as possible and pick you for your safety."

"If she gave me away, then I don't want to meet her."

"That is not how it works, my dear. If I keep you, sooner they will trace you down here. Come have your bath." He led me across the room. "I'll get a nurse to cater to those injuries."

I took a deep soak in a bath tub that offered no lasting relief. A nurse took my blood sample, disinfected my wounds, and wrapped them with bandages. When I stepped out of the tub and dressed up, Mr. Thompson reentered the room with a tall pretty lady I assumed his wife.

"Hello, Tabora. How are you feeling now?" he asked.

I flinched at the sound of so much cheerfulness in his tone, my headache intensifying. "Not bad. I want to find out if my boyfriend, eh, my brother, Mike, is still alive. Not knowing his state is killing me."

They both exchanged glances. No one spoke.

"Your wife?" I inclined my head at the woman beside him.

"No, Tabora. She is your mother. I asked her to come take you." His fixed gaze returned.

I sucked in my breath, and stared at the woman. Her face spread in a smile.

"She looks just like me when I was her age," the woman murmured, tilting her head to look at Mr. Thompson.

He nodded and she approached the bed and sat beside me. I stiffened as she drew me into a hug, her tears staining my neck.

"We named you Grace, not Tabora." She pulled away to gaze in my eyes. "Your father and I gave you a Christian name because we wanted you to grow up as a Christian child. But they took you from me to the community of your father's church. That is where they gave you the name, Tabora. The wound they caused in my chest when they took you still bleeds, the they took your brother, Mike, abroad to school, and my whole world shattered."

I held her hands.

"Grace," she called with a feverish earnestness. "I fought so hard to keep you both. You have to believe me. I did, my child." She withdrew her hands from mine, and wrapped them across her upper trunk. She rocked gently.

Mr. Thompson put his hands on her shoulder, and that calmed her enough to continue.

"Mr. Thompson and a few of your father's friends brought you back, but I had to give you away for your safety. I guess I was wrong." She looked at me with eyes that soaked with misery. "Life took you right back to them. Grace, I prayed every day so that you may find grace and favour with our Lord Jesus Christ, just like your name. I solicited that His Holy Spirit guide you aright." She wiped her tears. "Now you are home to your mother, where you belong."

"Tell Tabora the good news," the nurse turned to Mr. Thompson. "I will check back with the confirmation test in the evening before she departs with her mother."

He nodded.

"What good news?" I started out of the bed. "Is Mike alive?"

"We will know about that soon, Tabora. The news is that you are pregnant. The nurse will run a test to confirm how long you have gone. The blood sample she took was for that purpose."

"Pregnant?" My mother wailed, and her face crumbled. "Oh, Lord!"

I felt numb, glad to carry Mike's child but sad this child was my brother's.

"What are we going to do?" Mother asked Mr. Thompson.

"She is old enough to decide what she wants to do with the pregnancy. Whatever her decisions, I am sure we will stand by her," Mr. Thompson said.

"I am not leaving with you, mother." I drew back from her. "I am sorry, but I have my foster parents and brother. It will hurt my mum if I ran away." My chest heaved.

"Tabora, listen." Mr. Thompson's deep, solemn voice broke the silence that followed my announcement. "If you love your foster family, you will not put their lives in danger. The people after you are brutal. They will trace you to that home, and if

—

Mike is dead, Mrs. Elena might have already informed the community. Both the community and the police will be on your neck." He stared from mother to me. "Maybe your mother should tell you how hard the struggle was for her when she was falsely accused of killing your father, the things she had to deal with. Even though we did our best to hide and protect her, she still had to take wise and smart decisions."

The tension in the room thickened.

He continued, "You are old enough to take decisions, but if you decide to expose yourself, you will fight the government and the angels community all by yourself. Even if Rosy here wants to step in, I will not allow her risk her life for your stupid decisions." He walked out of the room, his cape flapping behind him.

Mother and I stared at each other.

"Grace, I understand how much you love your parents, but you must not put their lives in danger. The Adams are good people. I monitored your growth stages and ensured they were good to you."

"Yes, they are good to me."

"Do you remember your Aunt Esther?"

I smiled. "Yes, my mum's friend. She visits often."

Mother cut in. "Rev. Sister Esther is from the welfare. She helped in your adoption and monitored your growing up. I paid her to keep an eye on you, child. I knew all about you, up to your last relationship with Chris."

"You did?"

She nodded. "But I never knew when you got into a relationship with your brother." She wiped tears with the back of her palm.

"Don't beat yourself up. It is not your fault entirely. You did what you had to do." I sniffed.

The nurse returned to the room at about 6:00p.m. "Congratulations." She smiled at me, and turned to mother. "Call in Mr. Thompson, please?"

Mr. Thompson returned with mother into the room.

"She is only a month gone," the nurse announced. "Let me know when the decision is made," she turned to Mr. Thompson.

"We will." He gave me a pointed look.

The nurse came over to the bed. She checked my wound and added more Gentian Violet to prevent infection.

"How are you feeling?" Mr. Thompson asked me when the nurse left.

"Better," I said and then asked quickly. "Any news of Mike yet?"

"Nothing. I will contact the headquarters once you and your mother are out of here. Be patient. They might contact me soon."

As if on cue, the phone rang, and Mr. Thompson picked it up.

"Yes?" He paused. "Oh that is sad. It is okay. We will meet soon then. Thank you." He hung up.

"Who was that?" Mother asked.

"Headquarters." He frowned. "Mike is dead."

"No!" I could not breathe.

"Good Lord, no." Mother balled her palm into a fist and shoved it in her mouth, biting hard to suppress her pains.

Mr. Thompson spoke again. "But his body wasn't found, just like his fathers body isn't found till today."

"It is happening all over again." Mother sobbed. "This is exactly how they reported his father dead."

"The community set Mike's car ablaze as a cover," Mr. Thompson said. "They already reported to the police that he burnt in the fire. We will have to attend his funeral. I am so sorry both of you cannot come."

Mother shuddered. "Since that day my husband was reported dead, he never stopped telling me he is alive in my dreams. I can't deal with those dreams and the reality now that my son's body isn't found, too. It is a torment for a mother and wife not knowing if her loved ones are truly dead or alive. It breaks me every day."

She held out her hands and I squeezed.

"But this time, I am consoled that I have my daughter with me." She smiled.

I knew then that I could not leave her.

CHAPTER 10

My mother and I returned to her place at Nova Scotia, Canada, a residence with a long stretch of double acres and a big building with a tall fence around it. Mother lived on low profile with her help, and dogs.

Three months after settling in, I enrolled in a piano lesson to honour Mike's memory. I strummed the words of his letter in each key. Mike always boasted of being a pro with the keyboard, although he never played it throughout my stay in his secret hideout. I created in my mind a picture of him seated, with his fingers on the piano keys playing his favourite song.

As the days flew, the baby bump grew. My mother had a nurse come in every week to care for me and check the progress of the pregnancy. I felt strange that I was about to have a child out of wedlock but knowing I carried Mikes' child comforted me.

My piano instructor, Steve, was a big reason it felt easy-breezy for me. His voice, body posture and mannerism reminded me of Mike but the similarity ended there. Steve had a prosthetic right leg. He and his family were in a ghastly car accident on their way back from a holiday. He, alone, survived, though it cost his limb from the knee down.

The pang of losing our loved ones bonded us. I told Steve about the father of my unborn child dying in a car fire. If he felt I wasn't telling him everything, he didn't show it. He listened, and coerced me out of my dark moods. We went out for dinner a couple of times and more personal time to know ourselves better.

Mother contacted my adopted mum and brother through Rev. Sis. Esther. She invited the family over, a day before my child's delivery- a water birth at my mothers mansion. Everyone I loved was present and choked with emotions when my son entered this world on a Sunday at about 6:30p.m.

It was a February.

My son, his father, and I shared the same birth month. Tears refused to stop when I held the little bundle in my hands for the first time, and all I saw was his father, Mike.

"His name will be Mike," I said to all the faces gathered to welcome my child, and struggled to smile through my tears.

My foster family left a week after my son's christening. Mother promised I will return home when my baby was three months. Not to scare them with a brief on the happenings, we told my adopted dad that my son's father and his family died in an auto-accident.

Mother and I talked about moving to Nigeria. The plan was to stay at her parents' house until the heat settled. Mother was of a prominent lineage in Benin City, Edo state, Nigeria.

It wasn't an idea I was inclined to accept. Yet when I held my son, I knew I had to do all it takes to protect him from The Church Of The Angels and Mrs. Elena. I owed him a future, even if it required relocating to Nigeria.

Steve sent over a lot of baby items, more than we needed. He was floored by the news of my delivery, yet refused to come say 'hi' to my mother or see the child. His excuses remained endless. I did not want to force him, so I let them slide.

Steve's striking resemblance to Mike endeared him so much that he became a greater part of me. When I broke the news of our intended relocation to him over the phone, he wept. He said I was the only family he had and that the news broke him. I felt bad, but I had my son to protect.

Mother also informed Mr. Thompson of our decision, and he gave his blessings. He had been updating mother on the community's plans.

"Members are everywhere with keen eyes in search of Tabora," he said. "But we are covering both your tracks and ensuring no clues trace to you. We have done this successfully for years, and will continue as long as our services are needed."

"Thank you for all you have done, and are doing," Mother said over the phone, her cheeks turned pink with gratitude.

The Church Of The Angels was a spiritual organization fronting as a church. They were careful with their dealings to ensure nothing gave the façade away or brought the public sniffing around and pointing fingers. Though their deeds were coded, from what Mr. Thompson said, their tentacles spread everywhere and even right here.

"I think this move to Nigeria is a bright idea for now," Mr. Thompson concluded.

Mother was in charge of all the preparations. She booked our tickets, packed bags with essentials, so we forgot nothing vital.

All set, and only a few hours counting, I went searching for Steve a day before our departure. I wanted to give him the last opportunity to see my son and say our goodbyes. But Steve had left the piano training centre.

Another tutor, serving as his replacement at the centre, said he left a few weeks ago. I figured it was about the time I told him about our relocation.

I tried not to show my hurt around my son. The bathroom was a safe place for me to cry.

CHAPTER 11

The morning of our departure, I swung my son in the air, in a better frame of mind. I could not wait to start a new life with my two favourite people; my son and mother. I could almost smell the African soil of my great grandmothers.

Knock!

"Come in," Mother and I echoed together. Our eyes met, and we giggled like little girls.

A domestic staff walked in. "Excuse me, ma'am. There is a gentle man at the gate. He said his name is Mike and he is little Mike's father."

I caught my breath.

Mother was the first to snap out of her shock. "Did he say anything to you aside those?"

"No, ma'am."

"Okay, thank you," mother said.

The staff hesitated. "Should I let him in, ma'am?"

I cut in. "Can you describe him to us?"

"I can try."

"Go ahead, please," I ordered.

"Tall, broad shoulders, a tanned skin tone, with a deep voice. He spoke gently and appeared well groomed."

"It must be Steve. Please, let him in."

"Okay. The staff walked off.

Mother pulled me aside. "Why would Steve refer to himself as Mike? He should know that might hurt you."

I wasn't sure the sort of game Steve was playing. First, he left without notice and now, he got my attention by referring himself as Mike?

I was set to give him a piece of my mind. "Let us go see him, Mother. What time is our flight fixed?"

"2:00p.m."

We walked into the living area and my mother and I froze. Standing by the fireside, hands in his pocket, was our Mike. My Mike. Little Mike's father. My brother. My mother's son.

No one moved. Mother screamed and Mike ran over to catch her in time, before she could crumpled to the ground. He put a hand over her mouth.

"Do not scream, please.   The walls have ears, Mother." Certain she would not scream, he lifted his hand and set her upright. "Please, everyone, sit quietly. Let us talk."

Happiness at his reappearance, regrets of injecting him with the chemical concoction, all mixed emotions caused my eyes to brim. Mike kissed my forehead. He opened his arms and I gave him little Mike.

Mother broke the silence, still dabbing her eyes. "Can we all go to my room and talk privately?"

We sat in mother's bedroom, tears running down our faces.

"Talk to me Mike," I said, getting over my shock. "They lied to us that you were dead. I want to know how you are still alive. The news of your death made me carry the pregnancy to term." My tears gushed. "How do we tell little Mike that his parents are siblings?"

"Was that the reason you injected me with that chemical? You wanted me dead?" His lips tightened. "I wanted to verify your motive. That is what kept me alive. You hurt me the most, Bliss, attempting to kill me. But I forgave you when I found you, and then you told Steve of how much you loved me and wanted to keep the pregnancy as a reminder."

I hit his chest with my fists. "So you are Steve," I yelled. "Liar. All you told me about your parents dying in an accident was all lies. What else are you not telling me, Mike? How did you know we were in Nova Scotia? How dare you fake your death?"

He caught my wrists and stopped me from hitting him.

"Stop it, you two," Mother barked. "Grace, are you not happy your brother is alive? Please, pull yourself together. He has so much to tell us. I believe what he says will determine if we stay put or move." She hugged me. "Mike, tell us what happened, please."

"Mrs. Elena tried to kill Bliss and I. It was she, who attacked Dad and tried to kill him. She thought she succeeded, and framed you for his murder. But Dad is still alive."

"What?" Mother jerked. "When did you find out about this?"

"As soon as Bliss chanted the code, I realized she missed her words and became anxious on whose altar she would end up. So I tried to follow her with another code, but missed my words as well, from being too weak. I found myself in India, and guess whose altar I landed? Dad, practicing his own twist of our Angels and Indian religion. He heads his own church, but is not affiliated to The Church Of Angels."

"My God!" Mother's eyes widened and almost popped out of her head. "Is he really alive?"

"Yes, Mother. The moment I saw him, I knew he was Dad. He couldn't deny it either. It was an emotional few minutes of hugs and tears, after which he asked about you and Bliss."

"He did?" Mother asked, dazed.

"Yes. I spilled everything, told him it has been five years since I last spoke to you. He let on that you were in Nova Scotia, Canada, and asked me to come over and keep an eye on you. He was certain that if Bliss ended in any of his friends' altar, they will send her to you. So I transformed into Steve, my undercover self. The same Steve who accosted Bliss on the rocky path when she tried to run away from my secret house."

I gasped.

He smiled and continued, "You did not see my face clearly that night. Otherwise, you would have realized it was me at the piano training centre."

"We are about moving to Nigeria," mother said, her voice steadier. "It is 12:30p.m. now. I felt the move will be best for Grace and your son."

"You ladies should go. If you leave now, you might reach the airport on time." He knelt. "Bliss, forgive me. You are not only my sister, but the mother of our son. We can't fight each other."

I pulled him to his feet and clutched him in a hug.

"I actually amputated my leg." He pulled up his trousers to expose an artificial leg. "Thankfully, Dad had this Indian native doctor treat me, so the poison didn't damage more organs. Just my leg, every other thing is fine."

"I am sorry, Mike. I never meant for this to happen."

He shrugged. "Please, take good care of little Mike, mum and yourself. I will visit soonest." He hugged mother and turned to leave, but she held him back.

"Are you going to be fine, Mike?"

"Yes, Mother. Remember, a dead man has no troubles."

"Where will you stay?"

"I will return to being Steve once I hop in the car. My manager knows I am still alive, so my companies still run smooth. He introduced me as the Director that I partnered with before my death, so they know their new director runs the business."

"I am still worried."

He scoffed. "I will go elsewhere and start afresh, just as Dad did. I will come for Bliss and our son when all is calm. Meanwhile, I will visit, and I am sure Dad might reunite with us, because he never forgot about anyone.

CHAPTER 12

We arrived Nigeria Benin airport without a hitch. Grandma already had a taxi outside the terminal waiting to convey us to the family compound. The driver knew his way around the city and took the routes that kept us away from traffic. While he swerved in and out of the lanes, I stretched my neck to admire the ancient structures splattered in the mix of modern high-rise.

The ceremony that welcomed our arrival at my grandparents' family house could have been a replica of those wedding receptions I attended in the U.S.A. From the lavish decors and the countless dignitaries in attendance, I figured my grandparents were in the class of the country's elites.

Bedazzled in jewels, Grandma ushered us around, introducing us to other extended family members, dignitaries and celebrities. Some names stuck, others flew over my head as soon as she mentioned them. When the party kicked-off, servers thronged the room with trays of assorted traditional food. As though the festivity would never end, dignitaries trooped in till dawn, until I was exhausted and no longer able to flash anymore smiles.

The next morning, a meeting ensued with a few family members in attendance. Mother and I were ushered in to share our experience, and though we could not say everything, mother told them my Father and Mike were alive. She did not hold back on little Mike's paternity either. She told them he was Mike's son, a lovechild of both siblings, kept in the dark of their identity until after I was pregnant.

She admitted she got to know about the affair at about the time when Mike was reported dead, so I had to keep the child. But it turned out Mike is alive and dropped in at her place a day before we embarked on this journey. He told us Father was alive and hiding all these years. According to him, Father's reason was to escape the radar of his church members, whose sole mission was to see him dead.

Now, the same people want both his kids dead, too. Our lives were in danger, forcing us to move down here until the hunt fizzled. Mother ended her narration.

The family elders exchanged glances as if they already knew our story.

The eldest woman rose. "The child must undergo the Akobiç rituals, to tell the world he did not bring himself to the world, and hence deserves to live free," she said.

The others nodded.

Mother had an idea about the rituals, and being a Christian, she opposed the elder's decree.

"He will be dedicated to Osanuobua, the supreme, for total protection," the family head insisted, waving his hand-fan for emphasis.

Grandmother added, "And so should the parents of the child."

Tradition must be obeyed. They gave us no room to counter. They spoke a strange language and I missed out on a lot of back and forth that ensued between them and mother.

After the meeting dismissed, Grandmother came to our room and tried to convince mother on the need for the ritual. Almost in tears, she urged us to comply. We did not have the heart to decline anymore.

Finding a way to reach Mike proved tough. Mother had an idea. She sent a message to Steve at his office, stressing on the urgency of Mike's immediate arrival regarding little Mike's health. It did work as intended.

Mike arrived a day before the one set aside for the rituals.

The family head, Pa iEhiosu, also the family's Chief Priest, welcomed the new guest. Mother said the man was over 85-years-old and inherited the gods and shrine of his fore-fathers. Pa iEhiosu even had an altar in his house for other family members to worship. Grandma found it odd that he came himself to welcome Mike. She said he rarely does such.

Pa iEhiosu and Mike retreated behind the meeting room and spoke for hours. The old man spoke English fairly well, and soon, they reemerged in smiles.

The next morning, grandma woke everyone with incantations and incest smoke that filled the entire house. A group of ladies in white *wrapper* filed into our room and took little Mike to prepare him for the ritual.

They left behind white linens to wrap our breasts, same way as theirs, and reentered our room to decorate our fore-heads and arm with tattoos. Done with their chores, they requested we follow them on bare-foot, and led us to a car waiting in front of the building.

I caught sight of Mike in the passenger's seat, garbed in white cloth, knotted around his left shoulder and neck that left the right shoulder bare. He carried little Mike, naked and covered with white clay. We exchanged smiles before mother and I got in the back.

The driver maneuvered the vehicle to a small river in the outskirt of the village where some family members waited, attired in a uniformed red clothe.

The Family Head led us under a huge tree by the river bank where the other elders stood. The tree, with its diverse molded creatures and cowries décor, resembled a shrine.

Pa iEhiosu stepped forward. He held little Mike high above his head, and chanted incantations.

"*Akobię nwe,*" he chanted.

Everyone echoed his words.

"*Akobię omo owo. Olukun!* We greet you," Pa continued. "*Osannuobua!* We come to worship you. We brought the newest family member to you, and ask for your protection. He is our daughter's grandson. We came to say thank you, and did not come empty handed, but with food offerings prepared with our own hands."

The Family Head beckoned for the coolers of rice and drinks to be retrieved from the car boot and placed before the deities.

"We will not give you what we will not eat ourselves. So we will take some and eat."

Pa iEhiosu ordered all females to take a ration in a disposable plate and eat from it. He then prayed, took a cowry from the shrine and tied it to little Mike's hair.

He continued, "Unfortunately, the parents of our son here are the same blood. Akobię, our fathers used to say, 'children are precious gifts and shouldn't be

—

thrown away'. Both the parents and the child are our children. Should we throw them away because they erred? Or should we allow strangers harm them?"

"No!"

"Therefore we seek protection, *Olukun*, the giver of children."

Everyone echoed, "*Ise!*"

"*Olukun, ghe gie òmo wu mwen,* Olukun, do not let me lose a child," he said.

"*Ise!*"

"*Olukun*! A child is raised by all to bring prosperity to the household. *Ömo na ya mu nwa a ren*," it is with a child that one starts prosperity, he said.

"*Akobię nwe eee*," everyone intoned.

"*Akobię.*"

Mike and I were called to the river and ordered to kneel, with little Mike raised above our head. The elders, all garbed in red, cupped their palms and scooped water from the river. They poured it on little Mike, and some on Mike and I.

Pa iEhiosu took the child from us, and marched towards the elders gathered in a circle. He called for us to join the circle and, lifting the wailing little Mike, he declared:

"His native name shall be ogunbó, one whom the god of iron has favoured."

A few weeks after the ritual, mother's nightmares began.

One morning, she woke up screaming. "No! No!" And her howls had the entire house running to our room.

"It is Pa iEhiosu in my dream," she said to the anxious faces. "He tried to drown me in that same river we performed the akobię ritual."

"It is just a nightmare. Do not attach much to it," Grandma waved it off. "Olukun protects us, even in our sleep. Rosy, don't ever think iEhiosu would harm you. He is a great father figure to us all."

"We have a branch of our worship centre here in Nigeria. I will dial one of my pastors," mother said to me when the rest of them left, unsatisfied with Grandma's sermon. "He will have a better explanation for these recurring nightmares."

"You are hunted by leviathan, a marine demon," Pastor Akpan said through the phone. "He feels he own you, your daughter and her son. We have to pray a dangerous prayer, and command it to release your family. When that is done, you must rededicate your lives to Christ and stay off indulging in more rituals."

Prayer date was fixed for the 16th March. Mother and I prepared to take little Mike along with us. We told Grandmother we were visiting mother's friends at Akwa Ibom State, in the South-South of Nigeria.

That day arrived, and we successfully slid out of Grandmothers grip.

"You spirit of leviathan tormenting the peaceful dreams of this daughter of Zion, I command you, lose your hold in Jesus Name."

"Amen," mother and I chorused.

"In Isaiah 27:1, God slay you, and you shall remain slain. Whoever the son of God sets free, is free indeed. Hence, every covenant she made with you is today broken in Jesus name."

"Amen."

"I command your head to be crushed, just as in the Bible. Leave these bodies now." Pastor Akpan stretched his hand as if to convey an invisible power. The hand trembled, in combat with a violent force. "Out in Jesus Name," he yelled.

"Amen."

Mother and I collapsed on the ground.

I saw pa iEhiosu lead little Mike and I to the river in a reenactment of the ritual. We were dressed as on the day before but, this time, I refused to go with him. I grabbed my son from him and ran towards the car. The old man kept pace until he caught up and struggled to drag me back. He almost succeeded, but mother shoved him, a push that sent him tumbling down the hilly path and into the river. Not waiting to see whether he broke to the surface, we hopped into the car and zoomed off.

I opened my eyes. The pastor and mother were praying over me.

"Thank you, God, for the victory." Pastor Akpan lent me his hand and pulled me up.

Mother picked little Mike, asleep in his outdoor crib, and she folded up the cot.

"Be seated, you two, please." The pastor waited until we sat. "Now that Christ has given us victory, will you be willing to re-dedicate your lives to Him?"

"Yes," we both said.

He closed his eyes, and clasped his hands. "Repeat after me, Lord Jesus, we accept you as our Lord, Master and Saviour. Satan, you have no more place in us. Thank you, Jesus, for salvation."

We echoed a repeat and thundered an "Amen."

I felt lighter, free.

"Call me once you guys get home. God is with you," the pastor said as he walked us to the car.

CHAPTER 13

"Rose, before you left this family to study abroad, you knew our tradition and culture. You are no stranger to your people and gods. Why do you bring a strange God and spirit to combat ours?" Grandma's voice lashed like a whip

Mother sighed. "Why are you bringing damnation upon yourself and us?

"This conversation, my daughter, Rosy, is my warning to you. Stop whatever you are doing with that strange God." Grandma's voice trembled with restrained rage.

I spoke up. "But Grandma, she did nothing wrong . Are we not allowed the freedom of worship here? I need to know."

"Grace," now she sounded exasperated, "you are no longer a child, but a mother. I understand you are ignorant of your mother's family or tradition. But your mother is aware of what we accept or do not accept, our beliefs, who we worship, who our ancestors worshipped before us. She has no right to twist our tradition, or bring another god into this family other than *Olukun*. As a mother, how would you feel if your son acts this way when grown?"

"But Grandma-"

"There is no but."

"My mother has done no wrong in praying." I didn't let her hush me.

"You will understand soon." Grandma stormed out.

"Come over here, Grace. Bring my bible, let us pray," mother urged.

The room faded . . .

"Tie her up and throw her in there!" an urgent voice commanded.

"She will drown, please," it is Grandma's voice.

"Do as you are told, old woman. Or you want to go in her place? Come over here you two, and help Mma Emotan tie her up. Make sure both hands and legs are properly roped," the first voice instructed.

I fought them, tried to keep them back from touching me. Grandma watched and did nothing.

"Mummy, help me. Grandma, please, help."

"Your mother is not here, Grace. She dragged you into this and you will be an example to warn her further," Grandma said in a strange voice.

"Grandma, please. Why kill me to punish Mother? What about my son? Think about him, please."

"Take her to the river," the first voice ordered.

"Leave me alone. Help me, Mike! Where are you, Father?"

"Hold her legs. We lift on the count of three," one of the men directed the others. "One, two, three, lift."

"You cannot touch a born angel. You cannot kill a dark angel's spirit in her sleep. Let her go," a creature, with more hands and tails than I had ever seen, roared.

"We are just following orders," one of the men said.

"Put her down."

"We will return her to the spot we picked her from. But the old woman brought her." He pointed to Grandma.

"You brought her here?" the creature howled as he stormed over to Grandma.

She raised her chin, unflinching. "Yes, I did. She is my grandchild and will pay for both her sins and that of her mother."

"You have no right. She is my daughter, and neither her nor her mother will pay for any sins. This is my warning to you." The creature twitched and slapped his tail across Grandma's face.

The old woman fell to the ground, turned swiftly and cried out. "The mighty one, owner of the sea, help your daughter who is attacked before you."

The ground trembled and the waters rumbled. A huge anaconda rose from the river and charged at the creature that was my father.

I struggled to untie myself with my teeth, eyes on Grandma on the ground and watching the anaconda and the creature wrestle.

I untied myself.

"Help me, God," I wailed, certain that if the creature goes down, I was the snake's next meal. "Help me, Jesus!"

"Grace, are you okay?" Mother's voice called. "Wake up! You are having a nightmare."

I sat up in bed, heart pounding, drenched in sweat.

I struggled to speak. "Yes, Mother. It was a terrible dream and so real. Grandma tried to kill me."

Mother hugged me. "There's no power on earth, in heaven, under the earth or in the seas that is stronger than our God."

Knock.

"Come in, please," mother said.

"Good morning to you two," Grandma greeted.

"Good morning, Mother."

"Good morning, Grandma."

"Hello, Grace. Did you sleep well?"

"Yes, I did. Did you?"

Grandma smiled softly. "I always do. Your father was on the phone just now. One of the domestic staff picked. She couldn't get to you, as none of you were awake that early. He will visit in two days and is eager to see everyone, especially little Mike."

"That's great news. Isn't it, Mother?"

This meant one thing. The snake did not kill him in the dream.

CHAPTER 14

Father's plane landed.

For the first time in my life, I would see my biological father. I had no clue what he looked like, sounded like, or how he smelt. I didn't know whether to be excited or nervous. Would he like me? Would I fall short of the image of me he carried with him all these years?

I had no place for anger, for abandoning us and mother all these years, separating our family. None of that mattered. I had a new lease on life, to begin afresh, get to know him, and I would not let anger destroy it.

The entrance door opened and the servants brought in several luggage, then my father entered, the afternoon sun behind him. After the servants departed and shut the door behind them, the light cast his face in the shadows. But I could make out the outline of a tall, muscular man in long sleeve shirt and a pair of jeans trousers.

"Welcome to Benin, Peterson." Grandma's voice rang calm, collected. "The last time you visited was for your traditional wedding to my daughter," she teased father like an old friend with whom she just reunited.

"It is obvious he had nothing to do here in Benin after that." Pa iEhiosu flashed a smile, and stepped forward, arms spread to embrace the guest.

"Thanks to you two." Father laughed, a thick, rich baritone that shared a similar ring with Mike's.

The man stepped into the light, and his features showed; lean, jaunty jaw line, sharp eyes that missed nothing, low-cropped hair, and a solemn demeanor on an intelligent face. The source of Mike's humour and friendliness now lay obvious. Father and Mike were a younger and older version of themselves. I had no physical resemblance to the man, my features were mainly mother's. While little Mike was the youngest reflection of both Mike and father. The male gene was strong.

"Bring my grandson to me, Rosy." Father held out his hand, his face aglow with excitement.

Mother took the child from me. She gave me a soft smile to let me know that it was all right, and passed him to father. Saliva choked me. My baby was meeting his grandfather for the first time. The emotion was too strong, too powerful. I felt tears burn behind my eyes.

"Grace, come give me a hug," Father said and made room for me in his arms, next to my baby.

The reception laid out in honour of father's arrival equaled a royal event and rivaled a comedy club. Despite being in a strange environment he had long visited, he stole the show. His sense of humour had even the domestic staff, who saw to the food and drinks, laughing hard and wiping tears with the back of their hands.

The feasting, dining and merriment continued till late. Everyone was exhausted and the family needed a quiet time on their own.

That evening, my father walked into the room mother and I shared for a private meeting.

"Grace, your mother and I have agreed that both of you, including my grandson, should leave this family house," father spoke in a solemn tone. He sat cross-legged on a high-back chair facing the bed. "We thought a relocation to a different state is preferable. Your mother picked Uyo, Akwa Ibom in the South-South of the country. The region is her pastor's origin."

I stared at him, not wanting to go on the run again.

"I suggested Lagos or Abuja, the country's capital, but she insisted Akwa Ibom was better for her," father continued, watching my face. "Your opinion is needed at this point."

I cleared my throat, and took my time to gather my thoughts. I did not want to sound selfish. "Father, I support the move, given the confrontation between grandma and mother, and mother's unending nightmares. I had one a few days ago and would not mind staying wherever she is safer."

"That settles it then." Father exhaled as if he had expected me to kick against the idea. "I will break the news to your mother, Rosy. Meanwhile, I hired an agent to get you two lovely ladies a nice flat and some domestic workers to help you settle in. He interviewed them, and picked a few to help you run the house and care for the child. Later, we will inform Mike about this and let him have the new address."

"Father, I do not think we should give Grandma and Pa iEhiosu the address."

His lips stretched in a tight, knowing smile. "Leave that to me, Grace."

I got off the bed. "Please, excuse me, I need to feed little Mike."

I walked out of the room and into the next room from where I eavesdropped.

"Rosy," dad's voice spoke up," I think we should come together as one family."

"What about the family you have in India?" Mother's voice was cold, angry.

"I have none, Rosy." Surprise clouded the voice. "I already have a beautiful family, a wonderful wife I love dearly, and two kids. How can I think of having another family?"

"But you abandoned us." The chill in her tone remained.

"True." Shame tainted this admission. "Until Mike appeared on my altar out of the blues, I never wished to return with my troubles. I felt that I and The Church of Angels had given you and the kids enough trouble. That is the reason I am ready to fight them now, to fight for my life back."

"And how will you do that?" Hope cracked the ice in mother's voice.

"I will return to the headquarters, let them know I am still alive, and then denounce their membership." His chair shifted, and footsteps moved. "Please, Rosy, assure me when all this is over, you and I will be together. Promise me."

"Promise you what?"

A hesitation. "That you will be with me forever."

"I have my fears, Peterson. What if . . . God forbid. I can't even say it. Instead of the Headquarters, why not come to meet my pastor? Accept Jesus as Saviour, and we will live here in Nigeria. I do not feel okay about you going back." Mother's voice shook as if about to cry."

"If I do not confront these folks, I will hide forever." Father's voice hardened. "I can't live that way, Rosy, not after seeing you, Mike, Grace and my grandchild. I have to stand as a man. I got entangled in this mess while in search of solutions.

"Solutions for what?" Mother asked, now curious.

"It all began with Pa iEhiosu," father said. "With one question. This is how it happened, Rosy."

"Are you sure you want to marry our daughter, Rosy?" Pa iEhiosu asked.

"Yes, sir, that's why I came all the way from America to Nigeria. We have been friends since I met her in school. I will do anything to marry her."

The elders laughed.

"That is all I wanted to hear from you, Peterson," Pa iEhiosu said. "Before you return to us with your parents, you will follow us to our shrine."

"Shrine?"

Pa iEhiosu nodded. "You will repeat these same words you told us to our deity, *Olukun*. This family worships the gods of our ancestors. Since Rosy's father is no longer alive, the gods must approve before we proceed. Do you agree to this?"

"Yes, sir. I agree."

"Good." Pa nodded and twisted a smile on the corner of his lips. "Come with me."

He led me into a different room, and my eyes popped at the things I saw; a gigantic African masquerade mask with weird feathers on it stood in the middle of the room, other smaller molded creatures circled around it.

Pa iEhiosu closed the door behind us. Then he raised his hands. "*Olukun*, we come with great news. We did not come empty handed because we are not sons of damnation, so we brought kola and gin."

He reached into a bowl in front of the mask, took a kola nut and broke it in pieces. He tossed a few lobes to the ground for the deity, and chewed on a piece. He opened the bottle of Roman rock dry gin that father brought, sipped to clear his throat, and poured a few droplets on the ground.

"Our great news is that this young man, Peterson, has come to ask for our daughter's hand in marriage," Pa iEhiosu intoned. "He agreed to join the family in worship of you. You have one more convert," he added.

"Excuse me. But I-"

"Quiet!" Pa iEhiosu snapped, his eyes flashing. "We brought him to repeat before you what he told us. *Udin non gha man egho; ovbie okherhe re na ron ren.* The palm-nut that will blossom into an evergreen palm-tree is spotted when it buds. Now, Peterson," his voice hardened, "tell *Olukun* what you told us."

"That is what happened, Rosy," father said. "Your uncle and the others took me to a shrine to state my intent. I did not know they initiated me until the nightmares began after our marriage."

"I still remember you screaming every night," mother said, her voice thick with tears.

"The nightmares were about your people. Most times, they dragged me to the river for some rituals. I confided my woes in my senior friend, Anderson, an elder of The Church of Angels. He promised their church could help in this spiritual warfare. And that was how I joined them. You had no clue about my membership until later in the marriage." He sighed. "I wish I spoke to you instead. I have to fix this. All I ask is stay with me, Rosy."

I heard sniffs, and guessed they were both crying.

"Father, when will you return so we could be one family again?" I jerked the door open, and caught them pull apart in surprise.

"First thing, Grace, a flat in the new state, then I have to deal with important matters in India. Once sorted, I will be back with your mother and we will be one family," he replied.

His eyes shone bright with hope. I believed his words, marinated in sincerity.

CHAPTER 15

We expected our taxi's arrival to the compound at about 12:00 p.m.

Father called for a meeting of my mother's family after we packed our bags. When the members present filed into the room and sat, he cleared his throat and began.

"I lack words to thank you, Ma Ematon, Pa iEhiosu, and everyone." He clasped his hands in front of him. "I say thank you. You opened your doors and hearts, accepted my wife and kids into your sanctuary in their distress."

"This is Rosy's home, too," Grandma said. "She is always welcome here."

"But not all families would do this after their child is married off." Father winked at Grandma.

Everyone laughed.

"I called this meeting to inform everyone that I will depart today with my family to India."

Faint murmurs interrupted, then Pa iEhiosu spoke.

"You already made plans and booked tickets to leave today with your family?"

"Yes," father said.

Pa iEhiosu shook his head. "But you know the family's tradition. A thank you to *Olukun* and disclosure of your intentions, including a solicitation for journey mercies would be proper."

"There is really no time. Please, you all will do that on our behalf." Father reached into his pocket. "This envelope is for you, Pa. Here, Mma, this one is for you. Here is another two million naira. It should be shared amongst the other families and domestic staff. And this one is for the rituals." He gave the last envelop to Pa iEhiosu. "I know you can make *Olukun* smile and bless us even more," he teased.

A car honked outside.

"Our taxi." Father did not try to hide his relief.

"We have cars and a driver to drop you all at the airport." Grandma frowned.

Mother went over to hug the older woman. "Mma mma, you know how Peterson goes about his things. I call him Mr. Clown the times he acts without thinking."

Laughter followed.

Our journey to Uyo, Akwa Ibom, cruising with my biological parents, made me feel once more like a child. Their arms occasionally caressed my shoulders, now devoid of its invisible burden of so many years. Their eyes matched the one I had longed to behold, the beat of their hearts matched the rhythm of mine. Something ran in our veins, thicker. I was a half of them both.

I wanted the journey to last forever but in less than two hours, we landed the Obong Attang International Airport, Uyo. Seated in front of the airport shuttle, a flash of my nightmare ran across my mind, but I waved it off as the shuttle bus stopped in front of a building. Our new house turned out a one-storey, low-rise building with a small garden, yet our apartment was not as big as mother's house in Canada or Grandma's house in Benin. Situated in a newly developed estate, armed guards manned the main gate, alongside a serene and clean environs to top off the list.

It took us a couple of days to properly settle in. Dad stayed for a few more days and excused us to fix things at his base in India. He promised to return permanently when he was done 'fixing things'. A day I couldn't wait to see.

His departure created a little void, but Mike called to inform he would come over, and the news revived our spirits.

The excitement of having Mike replace Dad's absence lifted my heart, but soon his conversation wore me out.

"You know how I feel about you, Bliss."

"Yes, I do."

"There are no coincidences in life. Why do you think neither of us have fallen in love with someone else for this long?"

I looked away, not having an answer to that question.

"I have not stopped thinking about what we shared. I love you, Bliss. I want-"

"What do you want? I am confused, Mike. We are siblings."

"And we have a son together." His deep voice countered.

I put a hand to my forehead, trying to quell the pounding inside my head. "That was a mistake." I threw my hands up and let them fall miserably to my side. "I mean, I would not call little Mike a mistake, but the entire event should not have happened Now I know better, Mike."

"Oh, you do?" He pulled me to himself, lowered his head and kissed me.

My knees weakened and my insides melt like ice-cream in a hot oven. I kissed him back, yet my weakness disgusted me. This wasn't right, an incest, a taboo, but my need suppressed the voice of reason as he carried me on top the bed lamp stool.

He shoved the lamp to the bed, spread my legs and kissed my thighs.

Goosebumps sprout all over my body. I ran my fingers through his hair, combed it gently and moaned as his tongue slid into my hole and played with my clit. I caressed his hairy chest and our eyes met.

"Stop it, Mike." I lifted my left leg over his head and jumped down from the lamp stool.

God! What was I thinking?

Mike remained on his knees, his chest heaving from pent-up passion.

"Leave, Mike."

He rose, covered the distance and claimed my lips.

"Don't struggle with the feelings, Bliss," he murmured. "Let it flow."

Time stood still.

"I will see you downstairs for dinner," he said when he released me.

I stood there, breathing heavily as I watched him walk out.

Dinner time, I hurried to the table.

My stomach rumbled from the delicious aroma of the chef's Akwa Ibom delicacy that filled the dinning hall. I jumped on the dinning chair, opened the ceramic serving dish and got slammed with the irresistible aroma.

"What is this meal called, Mum?" I salivated, staring at the inviting chunks of meat.

Not interested in my question, she gazed at the empty seat beside me.

"Why is Mike not at the table with us, Grace?" mother probed.

I followed her eyes and shrugged. "Maybe he is not hungry, Mother. He is grown to know when he needs food and how to get some. C'mon, Mother, he is not my son."

"No need for the sarcasm," mother snapped and gave me a curious stare. "I wonder what happened between you two when I left for church."

"What do you mean?"

"Look, this is Nigeria. What you and your brother had is prohibited here. It is incest. Not in this house. Not between my children."

"You are raising your voice and I am not a kid. Nothing happened. Relax, so you would not raise your blood pressure."

"I am sorry if-"

"Oh, it is okay, Mother." I rose from the table and walked off to my room, hungry and hurt.

The rest of the day, I sat on my bed pondering on the circumstances surrounding the birth of my son, little Mike. It all started with meeting up a pen pal, turned out a lover or my brother. I sighed. If Mike thinks we are anything other than siblings because we have a son together, he was a funny fellow.

I fell on my bed, face pressed against the pillow. It didn't take long before I slept off.

Chapter 16

The Lord Highest Angel sat stiffly on a tall throne. He wore a white, hooded, oversized cassock that covered his head and left his face barely visible.

The other Angels arraigned on low chairs that formed a circle. They wore a similar cassock as the Lord, except for their uncovered heads. Blue stage lighting luminaries shone across the hall, illuminating two unoccupied seats in the middle of the circle.

One of the Angels rose. "Lord Highest, we have a special case tonight. Permit me to call on the accused two Angels involved in tonight's case to the court."

The Lord Highest Angel raised his hand. "You may proceed!"

"I call on Mike and Tabora to the coven," the voice echoed through the chamber.

From where I stood, I watched Mike march in, shoulders straight, head high. He walked to the centre and took one of the seats.

"I call on Tabora to take her seat in the coven," the clerk's voice cracked like thunder, compelling me forward.

I tried to still my steps but failed. At the centre, I took my seat beside Mike.

"Now, Lord Highest," the angel looked up at the throne, "permit me to call on the plaintiff."

"Proceed."

He bowed. "I call on Angel Elena to come forth."

I jerked forward, and through the corner of my eyes, I saw Mike lose his calm demeanor for a startled expression. I never imagined I would come up against Mrs. Elena as my plaintiff.

Silence reigned as if at the law court. Everyone stood still until the Lord sat on his high chair. Two angels sat on either side of him with their scroll and quill, noting down every spoken word. Mrs. Elena approached the Highest Angel, bowed, and turned around to face the circle.

"*Ala vete hu.* The shadow is cast," the announcer's voice bellowed.

A shadow whirled, crushing me until I could not breathe, and then the presence faded.

The Lord Highest thanked the shadows for its presence. Then the bench clerk proceeded.

"Angel Elena, let us hear you."

Mrs. Elena bowed again. "The Highest Lord, these two in the coven should be persecuted."

"Why? Are they not our blood? Are they not fellow angels?" the Lord roared.

"According to *The book of the Angels,* if an angel betrayed, cheated, or posed a threat to the life of another angel for no just cause, such should be persecuted."

"Correct," the Lord Highest agreed.

Mrs. Elena raised her chin in triumph. "They have done to me worse, and even faked their death to escape repercussion, just like their father. I discovered," she pointed at Mike, "that he is alive. So I brought them here for justice which I know will prevail tonight, Lord Highest."

"Angel Mike, what do you have to say? You heard those accusations against you," the clerk said.

Mike rose and bowed. "Lord Highest, I should be the one bringing this woman here, but I did not. She has committed several offenses against my father, mother, myself and my sister." He inhaled.

"What is her crime?" the clerk asked.

"My father, elder Peterson, took her and her daughter into our home. He trained her to become a chef, employed her, and paid more than she could have earned, plus he saw her daughter through school. What did she do in return? She threw herself at my father, tried to lure him to marry her, but he only wanted to assist her and her kid. My father married my mother, igniting Mrs. Elena's rage and she killed him."

The Angels muttered amongst themselves.

"Yes!" Mike screamed. "She confessed to this the night she tried to kill my sister and I. My only crime, after my father passed, was to retain her. I paid her more than she earned under my father. I also cared for her other kids. Again, she wanted me to marry one of her daughters. When she saw my sister, Tobora, now called Bliss, she mistook her for the lady I wanted to marry and tried to kill us."

More murmurs from the Angels.

"Lord Highest, I plead that she be persecuted for her offenses against us and as revenge of my father's death." He resumed his seat.

"Tabora," the clerk called, "you also heard Angel Elena's accusations. What do you have to say in your defense?"

"What is this place? Where am I? Some kind of court or what?" I shot off the questions without waiting for an answer. "I do not know that woman. She tried to kill my brother and I. For Christ's sake, you can not persecute me. You do not have such rights. He, who is in me, is greater than you all."

"Sit down and be quiet, Tabora," the clerk cut in. "Angels, take Elena and Mike to the sacred room. Lock Elena in the tormentors' square. Let it torment her soul as punishment till the court reconvenes for a final judgment. As for Mike, lock him in the den of Rebellion. Let his soul feed on the book of the Angels so he understands who he is once again. Take Tabora to the rebirth sanctuary. She should be rebirth at once."

"You lie," I screamed at the approaching figures. My fingers clutched my chair. "You cannot take my spirit, soul or body. I condemn any tongue that rises against me in judgment, and I rebuke you in the name of Jesus Christ."

Like an astral projection, my spirit snapped back into my body in a flash of light.

I sat up in my bed, heart pounding against my chest. The heavy thuds lifted my upper trunk in the air and slammed me back on the bed.

"Mike! Mother!" I called.

Footsteps hurried down the hallway.

"Are you all right?" mother asked. "It is 6:00a.m. Nightmares again?"

"Bliss, is all well with you in there?" Mike's voice was heavy with worry.

My chest heaved. "No. Come over here."

They both entered my room.

"Clam down, Bliss. You are shaking." Mike's concerned face zoomed into focus.

I exhaled, relieved to see him alive. "You are in danger, Mike."

Mike scoffed.

"Let her speak, Mike," mother scolded.

I tried to catch my breath. "It was horrible, so real. I was at The Church of Angels in my dream, a court Mrs. Elena summoned Mike and I. She wanted us to be persecuted. But after hearing everyone speak, the judge, Lord Highest Angel, ordered for Mike and her to be locked up till a final hearing."

"Lord Highest?" Mike said in awe.

I clutched his hand, needing to share with him the fear of only a moment ago. "Yes, he ordered that I be taken to a sanctum for a rebirth, but I pleaded the name of Jesus Christ and woke up in my bed."

Mike stared at me blankly, lost for what to say.

Mother was the first to break the silence. "You both need to join me in our church's twenty-one-days fasting and prayers. The battle line is drawn, and we have to win with prayers."

Mike raised a hand to stop mother. "Woah, no one is joining you in whatever. None of us is in danger; and The Church Of Angels does not hurt her blood. We are-"

"We are what, Mike?" mother pressed.

I tried to get cynical "They don't hurt their own, but Mrs. Elena almost killed Dad, you and I. What an irony. Mother, I will join the fast. I have my son to protect. If . . ."

"If what, Bliss? I can protect my son, too. He doesn't need your useless prayers." Mike stormed out of the room and then stomped back in. "I am leaving this house first thing in the morning."

Mother's face darkened.

—

"It is okay, Mother" I swung my hands around her shoulders.

The following day, we set out for her church. It was my first time fasting that long, but the terror of my dream gave me strength and zeal to complete the slated days. At the end of the twenty-one days fasting, it was time for me to return to my adopted parents. I needed to give them the opportunity to raise little Mike.

Mother and I had a long talk about my decision.

"I understand, Grace. I called ahead to inform them, and they are excited about the news. God will protect you and my grandson. I will not stop praying for the family."

"Thank you, Mother."

"Flight 3724 AN to Uyo, Akwa Ibom State is boarding now," the page content announcer called on passengers boarding flight 3724 AN to get aboard. The boarding announcement echoed at the terminal.

I hugged mother refusing to release my grip. I must have squeezed the life out of her.

"It is time to hop on that plane, Grace," Mother spoke softly.

Until my plane left off the ground, I believe mother stood at the departure terminal unable to leave the airport.

Both my journey and landing were smooth. My foster parents already waited at the airport ahead my arrival. Mum called my phone immediately I turned it on, informing me of their presence.

My excitement over the reunion burned out when I finally saw them at the Arrival terminal. My body went numb, fear tormented me over getting them involved in the church of the Angels saga. Unsure whether I will bring them joy or harm, the horrific dream flashed in my head again.

Mum's voice reached me. "Hey, my baby."

She wrapped her arms across little Mike and I, kissed my son's tiny fore head and took him off the baby carrier.

My Dad came along and hugged me. "Welcome home, Bliss."

"Thank you Dad" my voice was toneless.

"Is everything all right with you, Bliss?" Mum frowned, she bounced the baby in her arms.

"Nothing, Mum." I managed a smile, threw my hand over her shoulder, and we walked to the car, leaving Dad to tag along behind with the luggage.

The rest of the drive home was quiet. Mum played with little Mike and Dad concentrated on driving.

At the house, my parents laid off all questions and allowed me settle in until evil struck, and paranormal things started happening.

Then they put on their invisible detectives' hat and clothed themselves with investigators' uniforms.

Chapter 17

"Bliss, we are your parents. We care about you. Please, tell us."

"Tell you what?"

"What happened when you stayed with your birthmother?" Dad asked.

"All went well out there." I saw they didn't believe me. "Why are you looking all frightened and pale?"

Dad ran a hand over his face, and leaned against the wall for support. "Your mother first experienced it. She told me about it but I thought it was all in her head or she was stressed and needed rest. But I started seeing *things*, too."

"Seeing things?"

"Experiencing things."

"Please, Dad, what are you talking about?"

He stood straight. "Yesterday I saw some shadow creatures glaring at me as I read the newspaper. Your mother complained someone touched her, whispered words she could not hear. She also heard thundering voices in little Mikes' room."

I shot to my feet. "Seriously? In this house? Wait a minute. Are you both insinuating all this has anything to do with my son, the other family or I?"

Father put a hand on my shoulder. "Bliss, do not take it that way. We want to help. All this started the day after you returned home. We wanted to hear from you, so we know how to deal with this paranormal happenings." He looked at mum for support. "Your mum and I agreed to bring a paranormal investigator into this matter."

I gaped at him.

"Will that be all right with you?" mother asked.

I had no reason to tell them not to, without drawing attention to myself. "Do whatever you need to do." I left them, my mind in disarray, not sure if I should tell them all that had been happening. I kicked the air. Seems my presence had endangered my foster parents. I glowered, until my head spun but the fright didn't go away.

I had to tell mum everything right away. I walked to the door of my mother's room, raised my hand to knock but froze. I was going to tell her the truth, that I was the bad omen, and all those paranormal activities might have been from the Church of the Angels. I do not want to lose my mum. I dragged my feet away from her door, back to my room and wept like a baby till I dozed off.

A harsh horsy voice woke me.

In the living room, I found my parents in the company of a team of paranormal investigators

"The night will be long," one of the paranormal investigators said as they walked around the living room surveying it. "What precise spot was the shadow creature seen?"

"Right here in the living room," father said.

"All right. We will mount our cameras, infrared temperature detector, parabolic listening devices and electronic voice phenomena scanner around the house to help the investigation." He clapped to get our attention. "I need every family member in the living room, please. All lights off."

We hurried to do his bidding. His voice trailed after us.

"To the earth and those who lie beneath. To the paths we are about to walk, and to those who tread them before us. To this home we have come, and to whom they once housed. To the new spirits or souls who just visited. Know we come in blessing and wish only peace. We have come only to know who you are and what you want." He cocked his head to listen. "My name is Tommy. I am here with my colleagues. The family is here, including Bliss and her son. We invite you to show yourself, talk to us. Why you are in this home?"

We waited.

"Who are you? What do you want?"

More listening.

"Everyone is here in the living room except my colleagues in other parts of the house. Do not worry, we will hear you through our devices. Just relax and talk to us."

"Someone touched me," Mother yelped, robbing on the goose-pumps that sprout along her arm. She held out her hand for the investigators to observe.

BAM! A crash.

"What was that?" The hairs on my neck stood on end.

"Sounds like something fell in the next room," dad whispered.

—

The investigator conferred with the other investigators through a walkie-talkie device and turned to us.

"A lamp fell off its stand," he said.

A door slammed. Mother and I held each other, both of us shivering like autumn leaves.

Father stood erect like a kangaroo ready to jump its highest. "I have a burning sensation on my left ear."

A squeal conjured from air and a man's shadow took shape in the dark. The figure, dark as a bad engine oil, quickly dispersed.

Everyone drifted to one side of the room.

"Thank you for your time," the investigator spoke into the air. "You have helped us with the answers we needed. Thank you."

We waited.

"Turn the light on," he spoke into the walkie-talkie.

The lights came back on.

"Mr. and Mrs. Adams, we will review what was captured in our devices; in order to evaluate tonight's investigation correctly. We will get back to you."

The other investigators entered the living room. They shook dad's hand and marched out of the apartment, tugging their equipments behind them.

None of us slept a wink that night, eager to know the results of the investigation.

The next day, the investigators returned to our house. They connected a few devices to a laptop computer.

"Mr. and Mrs. Adams, what you are about to hear will blow your minds, and you, too, Ms. . . . ."

"Bliss," I said.

"Bliss!" he repeated. "All right, everyone, put on the headphones, please."

He fiddled with his laptop computer.

—

"Did we all hear that?" he asked.

"That's one hell of a voice," mum jumped away from the device.

"Yes," the man said, "that voice was recorded during the investigation last night immediately I asked the question, what do you want?"

"Is it saying, I have come to take what's mine?" Father raised his eyebrows.

The man cocked his head to consider the question.

"I think it says, I have come to be with who is mine," mother chipped in.

"We thought it said, I have come for what's mine," the investigator said. "We all agree to have heard something similar to 'I have come' and 'what's mine'. We will allow the family to reason out what could be theirs or his." He rose. "We appreciate your contacting us, and will love to take our leave now. We consider our work done here."

"And we appreciate the outcome of the investigation," father said as he walked them out of the house.

"Bliss, do you still feel all went well at your birthmother's place?" Mum faced me squarely.

Mr. Thompson and mother had warned me about involving my foster family in the situation, that is, if I loved them enough. I could not open up to my mum without putting her in harm's way.

"Mummy, I still have no idea what is happening here." I feigned confusion.

"Or is there something you are not telling me, Adam?" She turned to dad who just returned from walking off the investigators.

Dad stopped in his tracks. "Darling, we have been married for over twenty-two-years. You were twenty, and I was twenty-one-years old when we got married. Since then, I have been open to you. How could you ask me such question?"

"I am sorry, dear. I think we should invite Father Mathew before this gets out of hands."

"Excuse me, Mum, Dad, can you figure this out without involving me?" I stormed out, leaving them staring after me.

Chapter 18

The phone rang.

"Is this the Adams resident?" the voice on the other side of the line asked.

I paused, debating between a yes or no.

"Yes," I said.

"Am I onto Mrs. Adams, please?"

I hesitated. "No. But you are speaking with Bliss, their daughter."

"All right, Bliss. This is Dr. Ward from the Accident and Emergency Department, White Cross Hospital, Austin Texas."

The room spun, airless. "Why are you calling this address from the hospital, please?"

"We got this contact from the wallet of a patient, an accident victim. We are reaching his family on his behalf. He is still unconscious."

The line beeped and broke transmission.

The phone slipped from my fingers and crashed to the floor.

Dad or my foster brother, Kennedy? Was this a prank call or linked to The Church Of Angels? Hot tears rolled down my cheeks.

"Oh, dear God, these people are innocent," I muttered wishing I had never met Mike. "Please, help me."

I paced the sitting room like a whale stranded on land, unsure whether to wait for mum to return from work or call her office. Maybe I should drive down to pick her. Or I could drive to Texas without telling her.

"Pull yourself together, Bliss." I bit hard on my fist.

I couldn't stay alone in here, running crazy. I drove to mum's work place, convinced her to come with me to pay a surprise visit to Kennedy, and we sped off to the hospital.

At the hospital, it was a struggle to calm mother until we met the Doctor. The dour face man in white ward coat told mum that Dad was involved in a gastric auto-crash.

"But what was your father doing in Texas, Bliss?" mother wailed, looking at me for answers that I did not have.

Dr. Ward led us to the ICU where we found dad in a coma, on his back with a cervical spin injury. The doctor said he may take two to four weeks to regain consciousness.

Mum snapped out her phone and put a call to Kennedy. He assured to meet us at the hospital soonest.

Throughout the five weeks that dad was in coma, none of us left his side for an entire day. I spoke to him about my day. Even little Mike, still learning to make sentences, had something to say to him.

"I love you, grandpapa." He kissed my dad's hand.

Mother stroked his skin and prayed her rosary. A period that helped us bond and cherished the moments we had as a family.

Father regained consciousness after a few weeks and was scheduled for rehabilitation after his surgery.

"What happened, Adam? You left for Texas without telling us?" mum asked in a hushed tone.

"Yes, Dad." I caressed his hand with my palm. "Not like you at all."

"Something is wrong at home." Father had a frightened look in his eyes. "I was hypnotized."

Kennedy had not been around all this while. He appeared lost. "What is wrong at home, Dad?"

Mum touched his arm. "Let your father complete his story."

Father winced as though trying to recall. "I drove out that morning on my way to work. A little way from our neighborhood, a man stood by the side of the street. He waved me and I stopped to give him a lift." He closed his eyes as if he avoided seeing the man's face.

"What happened?" I prompted.

He opened his eyes. "The man demanded I took him to Texas for an interview, and for some reasons, I couldn't refuse. I figured I could use the opportunity to see Kennedy. Along the highway, I turned to speak, but he had transformed into this giant creature with a tail. I had a panic attack and lost control of the car."

"I will send for Rev. Father Mathew as soon as we got home," Mother said.

I felt the blood drain from my face. Father Mathew might see through all this and reveal to my parents it had been all me this while. My head ached.

Maybe I will return to my birthmother in Nigeria or tell my foster family the truth. I was torn between two decisions as I glanced at my father lying dolefully on the hospital bed.

"We will discharge you today Mr. Adam," one of the doctor, on his rounds with other doctors and nurses, said to Dad after checking him. He scrambled on a medical chart.

"He can take the rehabilitation therapies from home at the centre I will refer him," he said.

"Thank you," mum replied.

Later, Doctor Ward came in to check on Dad. He okayed we could take him home today, but I was worried sick over the thoughts of what else, who next, is this even from the Church of the Angels? Why was my foster family their target instead of my birthparents? It was best Father Mathew came to our house to lift me of my miseries.

Two days after we got home, Mum invited Father Mathew over.

The Reverend entered in his white priestly vestment and a narrow strip cloth draped around his neck. Two small altar boys walked behind him, both in their ecclesiastical vestments. One of the boys carried a tray of Eucharist, the other had an altar bell. A burning incense swung from the censer.

Dad, Mum, Kennedy and I were at the door to welcome them. Mum offered food and wine, but Rev. Father Mathew opted to perform the mass before taking anything.

"Let us offer prayers to the saints." He made a sign of the cross. "In the name of the Father, and the Son and the Holy Spirit."

"Amen," we replied.

"Grace to you and peace from God our father," he continued.

"And with your spirit."

He lifted his hands. "My brothers and sisters, let us acknowledge our sins and prepare ourselves to celebrate the sacred mysteries of Christ."

Everyone was silent.

"I confess-".

We all joined in the confession.

Father Mathew concluded. "May Almighty God have mercy on us, forgive us our sins and bring us to everlasting life.

"Amen."

He swung the incense twice over our head and returned it to the altar boy. He took the Eucharist, the bread, gave thanks and said, "This is my body, take, eat it in memory of me."

He took the wine, blessed it and said, "This is my blood which should be drunk in memory of me."

The priest gave the flesh and blood, bread and wine, to everyone. He took some himself, and we all proceeded to the table. Mum had set a banquet, we ate and drank and spoke about the church and the love of Christ.

When father and the boys left, Kennedy and I took to playing some games of Chess. Mother busied with little Mike and father glued to the news airing on the television. It was almost dawn when we retired to our beds. Then the nightmare I thought I was free from returned.

Chapter 19

"Where is my son? Kennedy! Have you seen little Mike? Mum, Dad!"

Heee hek hek. A whiny child's voice echoed in the dark.

Little Mikes' voice.

I set off, staggering in the dark without a torch. Little Mike's cries ordered my steps. I entered the woods without caring what I stepped on. I dragged myself farther inside the wooded path until the voice amplified.

I stopped and looked up.

My son laid on an altar with red candles lit around him. The heat from the candle made him whine. I raced forward, but the transforming angels, creatures with tails and lots of hands, same figures I see in my dreams, surrounded my son.

"I have come to take my son," I raged.

"We took what is ours and he is home. Unless you came for your rebirth, stop fighting your own," a disembodied voice thundered.

"I am not leaving without my son." I tried to move through them, but they threw me back so high I hit the ground. My bones creaked, but I managed to rise.

"In the blood of Jesus, give way."

A few of the creatures fell off. I pushed to the altar and hugged my son, still invoking the name of Jesus, praying He intervene and fight for us.

The creatures pranced in our direction. I quoted a portion of the bible that my birthmother often used.

"For the Lord your God is He, who goes with you to fight for you against your enemies, to give you the victory, Deuteronomy 20:4."

In a flash, I was back in my bed.

I looked around the familiar room and laughed hard, thankful it was a dream.

"Thank you, Jesus, for the victory." I jumped off the bed and ran to little Mike's room where I found him sleeping peacefully.

I felt his pulse, found it steady, and whispered, "The devil is a liar."

It was 3:30 a.m. when I returned to bed.

The day was quiet as Kennedy readied to resume schooling at his base.

"Call me once you get to Texas," Mum requested as she hugged him.

He waved and entered the back of the taxi. At about 1:30 p.m. that day, he called to announce his safe arrival at Texas.

Nothing could go wrong today.

We had dinner at 6:00 p.m. and sat back to watch a little TV when the knock came on the front door. Then the bell rang.

"I will get the door." I stood from the sofa.

Mother glanced at the wall clock. "It is a little late for a visitor. Let us get the door together, Bliss.".

I found a man in police uniform at the door.

"Good evening, ladies." His hard face did not break a smile. "I am inspector Bright, from the state CID. We got a disturbing call from Texas that led us to believe your son, Mr. Kennedy, attempted suicide." He raised a photo of Kennedy with blood stains all the way from his neck down.

"Kennedy can never do that." My voice trembled. I tried not to cry.

Mum tugged at the man's hand, almost snapping it off his shoulder. "Officer, where is he now? Where is my son?"

"He is okay, ma'am. He was taken to the hospital on time. His roommate found him and called us."

"Sir, can you take us there?" My arm around my mum's shoulder kept her from slumping.

"Yes, ma'am. Can you drive right now or will you rather join our vehicle?"

Mum and I looked at each other.

"Give us a minute, sir," I said.

Mum tapped my arm once inside, a warning sign to comport myself so that Dad would not suspect anything amiss.

I dialed Kennedy's cell phone, it rang but no one answered. I rang his apartment, no one picked. I fished out his roommate, Paul's number.

My blood pumped as if my heart connected to an electric blood pump. I felt myself a beat away from hysteria.

"Who was that?" Dad asked.

"Jeffery, his wife went into labour this night," Mum lied. "Will you be fine all by yourself and Little Mike? Bliss and I need to get over there to assist."

Dad wobbled, not liking the idea.

"But he should have called the ambulance instead, or he should have-"

"He has but her condition is really bad," Mum cut in.

"Okay. I guess you ladies can go," Dad agreed reluctantly.

We hopped on the officer's vehicle for the trip.

At the Hospital, mum almost fainted at the sight of Kennedy lying on a bed with an oxygen mask.

"Doctor, what happened?" I tried to put up a strong facade.

"Let us step into my office and talk, please." The doctor led us into his office. "Have a seat." He pulled out two chairs on the opposite side of his table.

He scrolled through his computer, looked up at us and continued tapping the keyboard.

"He was brought in here around 5:00 p.m. by the police. He suffered a penetrated neck injury caused by a knife stab. We were told he was self-harmed. In any case, the police will investigate that." He nodded and moved the mouse on the pad.

"Immediately, we commenced a laceration in the sub-mental area, but he swelled in that region, worsened to a respiratory distress. A neck ultra-sonography showed a hematoma in the sub-mental region."

He turned the monitor to face us, and pointed the cursor to a circled red mark on an x-ray.

"So we opened the sutures under orotracheal general and extended the incision by 1cm on both ends. After we drained the hematoma, we noticed a branch of the lingual artery had been cut. We legated the bleeding vessels. There was a small laceration on the anterior vallecula surface, but no other pathology. We contracted a drainage with a hemovac tube and sutured the cut muscles and tissues on both sides."

"Please, wait a minute, doctor. How is he truly doing, with all you have said?" Mother interrupted.

"Everything went well. He was resting when you saw him."

"Doctor, but those machines are still on him. How can he be fine?" I quizzed.

"He is on controlled oxygen therapy. He is doing fine."

"Thank you, Doctor. We have to leave early tomorrow morning and return later. Else his father will suspect. We did not tell him because he is recovering from a major surgery. Will my son be fine till we returned?"

"Yes, a side nurse is with him." The doctor gave us a reassuring smile.

Mother and I returned to the ICU ward to see him.

"Kennedy, how are you feeling?" Mother caressed his face.

He flinched. "I am all right, Mum." His voice came out raspy.

"But your voice is hoarse."

"It will clear with time, Mum," I consoled her.

"Police are investigating everything, son. Whoever did this to you won't get away. I knew this was an attempted murder. You are not suicidal." Mum's eyes misted.

Kennedy gave us an apologetic look.

"Don't tell me you actually tried to commit suicide, Ken." Mum's voice had a shrill note.

Kennedy looked away. "All through the journey back to school, I felt monitored. I got home and went about unpacking. Paul wasn't in, so I called and he promised to be on his way. I felt a migraine, a voice spoke. It ordered me to pick up a knife, and instructed me to do it. I struggled not to do it, Mum." He sounded broken. "I stabbed my neck and the voice ordered me to do it again. But Paul barged in on the fight, grappling alone with blood all over my body. He must have called the police or ambulance that brought me here, because I was completely controlled by that voice."

Mum and I locked gaze, lost for words.

"We might be in a lot of trouble. More than we are fully aware of, Bliss. It might be a devil of a problem," Kennedy said, and in his eyes, the horror of what might have been if his roommate had not stopped him.

My stomach knotted, and a fever reared. My conscience bugged me. I knew I had to get out of the room.

"May I use your bathroom, Kennedy?" I ran into the toilet, shut the door and sobbed.

I brought this on my family and I had to end it. Next on my mind was my brother, Mike, an insider and someone I could confide in.

CHAPTER 20

Mike seemed unhappy to see me. I had to look him up to end the calamity that befell my foster family. After I narrated the entire ordeal, Mike insisted I go with him to The Church of Angels and rebirth. He said I had to reconcile with them.

"That might be the solution," he said.

"Bullshit! Makes zero sense to me, Mike. "

"Whether you want to do it under compulsion, after your family members are wiped off or now they are still alive, is up to you. But you must rebirth and when it is time, my son will, too."

His crazed expression awoke the old spiteful feeling I haboured for him when he tried to lure me into incest at our mother's place.

"Mike! That will be over my dead body." My pent-up anger broke out in a rush. He was inconsiderate all of a sudden. This was Steve not the Mike I knew.

Unable to get the succor I thought looking him up would offer, I flounced back to my foster parents' house, frustrated and emotionally numb, I withdrew to myself.

"I have to go visit my birthmother," I told Dad after a few days of solitude.

"But, Bliss, you just got here about three months ago. Why do you want to go back to Africa? Do you want us to speak with your birthmother to know how she is faring?"

"Dad! She is fine." I snapped. "I spoke with her a few days ago. I really want to be with her. I need some time to recoup from all this."

His shoulder slumped in defeat. "Give us some time and I will inform your mother of your decisions."

"Okay, Dad. I love you."

"I love you more, Bliss."

Few months later, I returned to Africa.

Seeing my birth mother gave me a bit of hope, a ooze of fresh air.

"Bliss, the violent takes it by force," mother said, though happy to see me, yet worried. "You cannot keep running this way, and your foster parents cannot suffer for what they had no hands in. We have to see pastor Akpan at once."

I did not waste a second to agree, I needed a solution so bad that my pupils had turned red due to desperation.

"The lion of the tribe of Judah this battle is yours. Let every power of darkness tormenting you be crushed by the power that is in the name of Jesus. We declare judgment on every demonic power from paternal or maternal side or the ones they themselves invoked upon themselves. The light of God has entered every dark situation and gives light now. Amen," Pastor Akpan prayed for us.

Few days later, Father called to inform us that Grandma called India, requesting to speak with mother. Pa iEhiosu was found dead in his shrine. We were all requested to come to Benin for the burial.

The news did something to my faith in prayers. I wondered if the arrows of our prayers had struck the old man in his shrine. The battle was closer to the whistle of victory been blown and we, declared victors.

Three month after his demise, Pa iEhiosu was buried in accordance with the Biki Benin funeral rites. A seven day ceremony and first of its kind for me. Dignities thronged the premises, from traditional rulers to Government officials, Governors and even the OBA himself.

The first day, *Orhimwin*.

Pa iEhiosu's body, already washed and laid on the bed in his room, was embalmed by a traditionalist. Traditional singers sang folk songs to alert the neighbours that the burial process had commenced.

The second day, father joined all in-laws and male descendant of the family, dressed in white traditional attire, for the ritual of cow slaughter cooked in assorted meals. A feast ensued in the wake of burial songs that ran through the night till the next day.

On the third day.

Pa' iEhiosu's first son slaughtered another cow to appease the Edion, the departed spirit. Barbequed suya, the Nigeria flat beef, was the top of the day.

Cultural dancers took centre stage on the fourth day. A few elders, mum and Dad were in a meeting. Preparation carried on in the background.

Day five; *Isoton,* a parade in town.

All Pa iEhiosu's children, grandkids and his co-priests took to town in their traditional costume. Not wanting to miss the show, I joined the procession. They carried a wooden box, *Okun*, decorated with mirror on each side with red and white cloth and brass ornaments. Some of Pa's valuables lay in the box. They believed he had to give it out as his last philanthropic activity on earth.

The priests chanted, in communication with the deceased. The mirror on the box was believed to serve as a passage between the deceased and them, to direct on the spot to halt the procession. The procession ended at a statue site called Emotan, the same name as Grandma. Emotan was known by her generosity while alive.

Everyone offered a gift, and the box full of offering items was left at the statue site.

Day six was a wake- keeping.

All well-wishers, friends, family and attendees gathered at the compound, including Pa iEhiosu's grandchildren who rendered poetries about the deceased.

My senior cousin, Ihuanedo, was chosen as Eno-derhayi, the deceased's representative. He was not to fall asleep at the wake; else the deceased would take him to the great beyond. Everyone gathered around, filling him in with conversation to keep him occupied till dawn.

The seventh day, the day of casting away, *isuerhanfua*.

Cousin ihuanedo led the crowd into a nearby bush. He sat on an erected framework of sticks and everyone followed suit until the structure collapsed. He proceeded to a nearby river, stepped in it, and everyone did the same. He scooped some water and spilled on the sand.

Then ukhure, a wooden staff representing the deceased, was placed on his shrine, a goat slaughtered as offering- a part of the rites to send away the deceased's spirit. The traditionalist played cultural rhyme's with the *emaolukun* drums, *Ukuse*, a native maracas and *egogo* metal gong. The undertakers danced to the beat of the *Ukuse* and spoke with the *ogiuwu*, dead, all the way to the cemetery.

Only members of Pa's family were present when the undertakers lowered the coffin into the grave. Prayers were said over a handful of red sand and emptied into the grave by Pa Obaseki, the next family-head, the second oldest male in mother's family.

CHAPTER 21

The funeral was over but its effect remained.

It was at the ceremony that I met my prince charming, Adebayo, son of a prominent Doctor and politician, a celebrity Doctor. At thirty-five-years, he was Chief Consultant at his father's hospital in Lagos, Nigeria.

My cousin, Ihuanedo, introduced him at the burial as a friend and colleague at the same hospital. And we paired off instantly as if we had waited our entire lives for each other.

He was the perfect all-in-one package; ambitious, gorgeous and emotionally articulate. The way he wore his Apala when I first met him at the funeral cinched it for me, that Yoruba attire with its symbolism of the African talking drum.

It was not a love-bomb affair, though his love spiraled at top speed. We met a couple of times after the first intro and called on the days we could not meet up. Adebayo made the trip down to Uyo a couple of times and met my birthmother, gaining her approval of the relationship. She raved about his personality, humility and respect for others, but most importantly, we shared similar beliefs in regards religion, family and life.

Adebayo opened my heart, made me laugh again, gave me a sense of contentment.

"I am lucky to have you, Ade," I said in a solemn voice one evening just before dinner.

"I am the lucky one here." Laughter laced his voice. "Who would not want to have a lady like you, sweetheart? The depth of love you give your son and family captivates me. You are a gift worth celebrating, and I promise to always celebrate you." He trailed his fingers along my arm.

I smiled through my tears. "Thanks for agreeing to share your love with me."

He poured some more wine into our glasses. "Let us toast to that, sweetheart."

The candlelight dinner was at a quiet spot with a table set for two, and lit candlesticks formed a love-shape. My favourite seafood dishes; grouper with cucumber salad, stuffed crabs, grilled lobster tails with dip sauce and grilled marinated shrimps, jalapeno cocktail sauce, all cooked to perfection the Nigerian style, made up the menu. The wine completed the evening, a sauvigrion blanc, dry rose and pinot noirs to compliment the meal.

I could not recall most of what we talked about, but it drew us closer.

"I had a good time," I said, not wanting the evening to end.

"Same here, sweetheart." Ade winked. "Let's do this often."

Charming, in a fitted shirt and straight-leg trousers with a stylish sneaker, Ade was like those professionals with a touch of wittiness.

"We will do this again," he repeated as he walked me to the gate of mother's house. "I will lodge at Monty hotel tonight. I wish we were together, Grace, but I will wait till you are comfortable."

"I understand the feelings, Ade."

We hugged and he pressed the bell to alert the security. I watched him walk to the taxis as my gate slid open.

I had not thought of The Church Of Angels and its troubles since I met Ade. It had been eons since I felt such peace. Little Mike was growing fast. Dad returned to work, and Kennedy went back to school to complete his studies.

Mum said Paul, Kennedy's roommate, moved to another apartment closer to their university campus.

I was at total bliss.

CHAPTER 22

Our relationship bloomed.

Adebayo requested to meet my brothers, Mike and Kennedy, right after I met his family. Ade's educated parents had no problem with me being a half-Nigerian. Ade was their only surviving child. Their closeness reminded me of my foster family before I brought them trouble. Core-traditionalists, every family member in Ade's home knelt or prostrated to greet the elders.

"*Ė ku Aaro* maimi, morning, Mummy. This is the one I told you about."

The older woman's eyes dwelt on me. "She is beautiful, Ade. Welcome my daughter." She pulled me into a hug and patted my shoulder.

"Is she for your mother's eyes only?" Ade's father walked down the stairs.

"*E pele o, Baba mi.*" Ade prostrated. "*O dara owurö*, sir, Good morning, sir. *Eyi ni Olufę mi.* This is my lover."

"Good morning, Dad," I said

"Welcome. I see you have met my wife, Ade's mother, already."

"Yes, sir."

"Be seated."

Then the questions flew, and I did my best to keep up and gave my sincere answers.

A few months after that meeting, we travelled to the State to meet my foster parents and brothers.

Dad and Mum were skeptical about the cultural differences, but gave in after a little persuasion on my part. Kennedy's smiles said it all. He nursed a fear that I might never find the right man when he heard my son's father died in an accident. He and Ade bonded almost immediately.

Mike or Steve invited us over to his place. We arrived late in the evening. It was a smooth meet with a cordial discussion between both men, with occasional laughs and humour.

At the table, Ade prayed before meal and it was beautiful seeing Mike corporate with him.

"It is getting dark, Bliss. You guys can sleep over at the guess room instead of a hotel," Mike suggested.

"Thank you, but no." Ade turned down his offer.

"But this is my brother's house." I reached for his hands. "Please, honey."

"How can I say no to this angel?" Ade's broad smile revealed the dimple on his right cheek.

I kissed his succulent lips.

Mike observed us with a grin.

After we tired out watching television and chatting, Ade took his suitcase and we retired to the guest room.

But!

I woke up to the taps on my leg.

"Wake up!"

The voice reached me faintly, it was Ade's voice.

I opened my eyes to bright lights, similar to five stage luminous lights shining inside our room. Ade stood at the foot of the bed. He frightened me to death.

"Ade, what is it?"

"Hush." He ran to his fancy channel suitcase, shuffled through until he pulled out a small brown bottle. He emptied a powdery substance into his palm and blew it in the air.

"*Esú ódara, Riru ẹbo lo ngbe ni, Airu ki igb' enia.* Offering sacrifice helps a man, refusal to do so is detrimental. Although, I am in a strange land, I give you my offering *Esú ódara. Olódúmare, ebo ŕiŕu ló ngbe ni,* it is sacrifice that resolved issues. Something is about to happen here and I sense it. Redeem my lover and I from what is about to happen."

Before he ended his chants, members of The Church Of Angels appeared in our room, transformed into man-Scorpio- like creatures with tails and countless hands. Mike was not among them. I could recognize him even when he transformed.

Ade held me, his heart hammered at the sight of such creatures. Mike must have traded his soul freedom for my rebirth. I burned to fight them, feigned terror. I didn't want Ade to suspect I had any idea what the creatures were.

"*Olúdúmare*, help us, please." Ade screamed.

A giant in an all white garment, his head almost touching the roof, formed into a solid figure and sauntered into the middle of the room. The figure blew fire from his mouth, ears and nostrils. It came on Ade's summon.

The *Olúdúmare* apparition opened his mouth, spewing an endless stream of flames that consumed the creatures. Dark shadows flew out of the windows like kites. At the disappearance of the last of our assailants, the *Olúdumare* sucked up the bright lights and fire, and vanished.

"Ade, what just happened?" my voice shook.

"We had victory." He could not suppress the tremble in his voice. "I do not understand what those creatures were, but the giant is *Oludumare*; our Yoruba God."

My mouth went dry. I hung on Ade's heaving chest and didn't let go until we both felt asleep.

The next morning, Ade packed his suitcase, his chin set. He managed to smile a greeting, and then we went to the sitting room to inform Mike about our departure.

"Good morning, bro."

"Good morning, Ade. Why the suitcase, moving out early?

"I have to catch up with my flight."

"My sister will drive you to the airport. Is that right?"

"Yes." I still blazed from last night's rage, but kept calm.

"It was really nice meeting you, Mike."

"Same here." They shook hands. "Take good care of her," Mike said.

"That is all I live for." Ade gave a thumb-ups, a skaika greeting, common among Hawaiians.

Mike walked us to the car and watched us drive off his apartment.

CHAPTER 23

As soon as Ade boarded his flight, I phoned my birthfather and reported all that happened.

"You should have told me this earlier. Thank God the rebirth, or whatever their mission, didn't go through."

"But now they know about Ade."

Father hesitated. "Mike needs help. His soul cannot stay in their lock-room any longer. The more he is fed with the deep mysteries of The Church Of Angel, the more like them he becomes. I must go to the headquarters. It is time for a final battle. I have to end this, or it will affect my generation."

"But, Dad, you are no longer strong as you once were. Can I come along?"

"It will not be an easy battle. Lives may be lost. I will not let you trade yours for mine. Do you understand?"

The line disconnected.

Discontented over the discussion, I dialed my birthmother and informed her of father's decision to visit the Headquarters of The Church of The Angels. I told her how deadly he said the showdown could get.

Mother sighed from the other end of the phone. "Your father already shared that with me. I tried to discourage him but he remained adamant. All we can do is pray for him. I will fast and ask God, the Mighty Man of battle, to take the war front. Do not give Ade any reason to fright, okay? I love you, dear daughter. My regards to my grandson."

"Thank you, Mother. I love you, too."

The call disconnected.

I felt uneasy still. Father should not go there alone.

I called father to ask when he planned to embark, to enable mother and I pray, and he mentioned the date. I rushed over to Mike's convincing him I was ready to give my self for a rebirth.

"Do you really want to do that?" His face shone bright with excitement.

"Yes, Mike. It will be best. I need your assistance to get to the headquarters."

"But why the sudden change of mind?" He searched my face.

"I am doing this for Ade and our son. I do not want the church to haunt them."

I must have convinced him. He agreed to take me on my choice date.

When the day arrived, Mike and I took off to the headquarters of The Church Of The Angels early. We arrived the high-fenced premises but seeing Mike with me, we were allowed entry and some members led us to the sanctum.

They were prepared for the occasion, my rebirth, in a white chasuble. The altar was prepared with red linen, lit red candles surrounded it, and a platter of knife laid next to it.

One of the members gave me a red alb cloth to wear. I was led to the altar and laid face up.

Everyone waited.

The Lord Highest walked on air. He patted Mike's shoulder and proceeded to the altar where I laid.

"Avuuumm," he chanted.

"Avuummm," they replied, including Mike.

I felt groggy, but called on the Holy Spirit to bring father here in time.

The Lord Highest Angel invoked with a high pitch tone as if he struggled with an unseen power.

"Avuuumm," they repeated after him.

He raised his hands, shook his fingers as if conjuring forces into the room, and chanted again. "Avuuumm."

I intensified my prayers. "God, do not leave me alone."

He turned to me. "What do you think you are doing? Try that again, I will kill you and sacrifice your spirit to the dark shadows." He turned away and continued his chants.

My father appeared in the room with about ten members of his church in India, and the Lord Highest Angel guffawed.

"My long dead and forgotten elder. Welcome home and join us," he mocked. "But first, introduce these ones with you, and tell us why you brought them into my holy sanctum."

"This will be a very interesting introduction," father's words dripped sarcasm.

"Are you here for war, Elder?" Lord Highest did not wait for father's reply. He chanted, *"Chastu pu sa ti tum."*

All the Angels transformed into Scorpio-like creatures with long tails and hands. Now it was my fathers turn to introduce his company. A long vein resurfaced from his neck muscle.

"May I introduce to us **Shiva,** the destroyer of all obstacles," father said.

A creature with long unicorn horn protruding from its forehead, its tail like those of a scorpion and hands, appeared amongst his men.

Father continued the introduction. "**The elephant king.**"

Some of the men evolved into elephants with big body, hands, and elephant tusk on their face.

"Lastly, permit me to introduce the mighty **serpent god.**"

The rest of the men turned half-human and serpent. Seven smaller serpents formed a cobra hood on their head.

"Dad what are you doing?" Mike, transformed into a Scorpio-like creature, screamed.

The Lord Highest thundered "Veeeeedaaaaaaaaaaa!"

Darkness covered the building. I heard only voices, painful screams, stomping feet, hisses, bones cracking, teeth gnashing and murmurs. A hand schlepped me from the altar.

I opened my mouth to scream, but Mike's and father's voices spoke in an undertone. "Silence."

"Where did they lock your soul, son?" Father whispered, but loud enough for Mike and I to hear.

"This way, Father." Mike held onto him with one hand, while he carried me with the other hand.

We ran through a narrow corridor to a prison separated by a security wire. I heard screams from the sanctum, and a shrike of terror from souls locked away in the prison rooms.

"Here, Father," Mike said. He saw clearly in the dark.

The only light that shone was the brightness of father's eyes. I could not identify the nocturnal animal Dad had turned into.

Father said, "Mike, here is your soul."

Mike's creature body vibrated.

Someone screamed from the other side of the locked room, "They are here." alerting others.

It sounded like Mrs. Elena's voice.

"Hurry. Run, Mike. Take your sister home," father yelled.

Both men chanted in different tongues. Mike and I landed in his house.

Neither of us had any inkling what happened to father or would happen if he was caught there.

"I have to go back, Bliss." Mike was irked by the way we left without father.

I tried to make him see reasons, stayed in his face to stop him from making a hasty decision. Throughout that night, no one slept. Anxiety took the best of Mike, he tried to reach out to all father's church members at the headquarters with him. Mike had been to India and knew these people on a personal level.

Not able to reach any of them, he dropped messages. If any of them returned alive, or had an idea what happened to father, they would reply.

Still hoping, Mike called father's house-keeper in India to lock up father's room. No one should be allowed in until father called her.

The housekeeper and the other domestic staff knew Mike's identity.

Chapter 24

Mr Adesh, one of those who accompanied father to the headquarters, called us.

Mike jumped out of the chair, set his phone on speaker, as a voice said, "Hello, Mike, it is Adesh."

"I know," Mike answered, breathless.

"Sad to say, but your father was captured and locked up in their torture chamber. We tried to get him out but the risk was too much. We lost five of us. I had to get others to retreat. The families of those who lost their fathers mourn. It is a sad time for us all in our organisation here in India. Moreover, your father's soul is still alive, but his body sleeps as if in a coma. It is your choice to either rest him or allow him stay in coma until we can recoup for a second battle to free his soul."

"Did you say rest him? Like kill him or bury him? You and I know he is still alive. I cannot kill my father. I will go back tonight and get my father," Mike swore.

"You will not do anything unthinkable, son," Adesh scolded.

"You are so unreasonable, Mike. You will do no such thing," I rebuked.

He clenched his fists into a tight ball, and kicked his leg in the air. "Then what should I do, Bliss? Should I wait and do nothing?" He stomped like an elephant.

"Adesh, how long will it take for your people to recoup?" I enquired.

"About a year or ten months," he replied. "Calm down, everyone. We can also seek alternative solutions from other entities. We just have to find one who is willing to join forces with us. Meanwhile, get a nurse who will care for his body."

The line went off.

I picked up my phone and dialled Ade's number without thinking.

"Hello."

"Hello, sweetheart."

I pressed the phone to my ear. My mind went blank.

I discontinued the call but he called me right back.

"Is everything all right over there? Please, talk to me, sweetheart."

A tear dropped. "It is father," I said

"What happened to him? Which of them?"

"My birthfather in India. He is in a coma. But that is not the challenge, Ade, he slept and could not wake up anymore, but he is not dead."

"Hypnagogic sleep paralysis?"

I said nothing. It was not medical.

"It is okay, sweetheart. We can go and see him, if you want," Ade said.

I sucked in my breath. "It is a supernatural tussle, like what you witnessed in Mike's place."

Ade was silent, then he said in a flat voice. "They attacked him, too."

"We need to go and bring him here."

"I know a powerful spiritualist, who can help. He will get him fully recovered. He communes with the supernatural and spirits of the dead."

"That will be nice, Ade." I felt relieved.

"But you need to get Mike to agree with us on this. Then we can proceed."

"Okay, let me see how I can get Mike onboard. Thank you so much, Ade."

We ended the call.

It was not easy convincing Mike to buy into our idea but finally he did.

We travelled to Mumbai, India, and proceeded to father's room where he laid as if sleeping. The hired nurse took great care of his body, cleaned him so he didn't have bedsores. He had a catheter on him and tube linked to a ventilator just as a comatose patient should.

Mike inserted another tube, the tracheotomy, to enable us move him to our ambulance flight back to Nigeria. The flight had intensive care equipment and specialist on board.

Ade had all the documents for a medical repatriation and everything were in order.

CHAPTER 25

In his thatch hut, the Yoruba Diviner, *Babalowo*, chanted;

"*Àkúnley àné da. Òun làdáyéba. A dàyetán ojù n kán ġboġbo wa. Sù ğbóṇ éđ ànàá kò leè padà lö yan. Òmoran. Àfi ètùtù lò ku.*"

I interpreted it to mean;

What was chosen kneeling down, is what we find on arrival in this world. On arrival, we became impatient, too much in a hurry to achieve our potentials. But it is impossible to go back and chose another. Now, to prevent the deterioration of things is the only course of action left for us.

The *Babalawo* laid father on a mat, his back to the ground. He placed leaves, herbs mixture, and bird feathers from father's neck down to his feet. It chilled me to see my father so still, unmoving, almost lifeless.

Oblivious to our anxious silence, the diviner continued his chants;

"Ifa, our great oracle, we greet you. We bring before you the body of a man whose soul is taken by his enemies. Great Ifa, a man can only be complete and alive when his Ara, body, houses his *Emi*, spirit, and *Okàn*, his soul. This man is half-dead. Whether his situation is caused by *àje*, witchcraft, or *Òrisa* gods or *ebǫra*, our ancestors, or enemies bearing grudges, or rival occult groups, I ask you, take me there to free his soul so it can return to his body."

From the inner chamber of his hut, he pulled a black goat, dragged it over to the spot father's body lay, and slaughtered it. He collected the blood with a calabash, sprinkled some on father's fore-head, invoking strange spirits.

The *Babalawo* picked a piece of stick off the floor. He scribbled on the sand, his hand moving fast as if controlled by a spiritual force. After about an hour, ours eyes getting dizzy following his hands movement, he stopped.

He lifted his head, as though just realizing we were still there.

"Your father's soul will be released on one condition," the corner of his eyes crinkled as he continued, "a human sacrifice shall be offered to the dark shadow spirit, an atonement for their members killed during the battle your father caused."

"But-" Mike broke off. The strange request rendered him speechless.

"There is no 'but', son. There are no options here," the diviner said. "We must do it and fast before the affixed day for his soul's execution."

"Execution?" I was not sure I heard right.

Fear choked Ade and Mike, both of the too silence for comfort.

"Yes. In the vision I saw, his soul is marked for destruction. We must appease them fast."

I shuddered.

Ade found his voice faster than the rest of us. "But where would we get a human for the sacrifice, Baba?" He clasped his hands in a beseeching gesture.

"If you lack the stamina to get it yourself, pay me one million Naria to get that on your behalf." The Baba's voice remained impersonal. "Once the ritual is completed and accepted by the dark shadows, your father will be freed."

My body felt cold. I could not believe I was in the same hut, talking about taking an innocent person's life as though it was merchandize.

"No way, we will not do that, sir." I would not taint my hands with human killing or sacrifice or whatever he chose to call it. I would not allow my brother or lover shed innocent blood just so another can live.

Mike and Ade scooted close to me.

"Excuse us, Baba," Ade pleaded. He turned to me. "Sweetheart, your brother and I will not take another's life, but we will give him money. He may not use it for that purpose. Just let him continue his job. All we need is that your father's soul returns into his body."

I looked at Mike, he nodded.

"Okay, Baba," Mike said, "we will get you the cash tomorrow."

Baba frowned and tossed a handful of cowries on the floor near the scribbled writings. Another round of chants ensued. He picked the cowries, blew air into his cupped palms and tossed again.

"Be here before 6:00 a.m. tomorrow. Leave your father in the shrine tonight," he said.

Mike lingered, reluctant to leave father's body behind. With nothing else to improve the situation, we trooped to Ade's place. Mike paced about the sitting room. He insisted on returning with the money that evening but we dissuaded him.

He finally agreed to wait till morning.

No one slept fully through that might. Mike and I were anxious to see what will happen next after payment. The sacrifice might work or the man will be exposed as fraud.

Before dawn, we were on our way to the Babalawo's hut with the money in the back seat. We drove like the devil was after us and arrived at the shrine before 6:00 a.m.

Not trusting the Diviner, Ade put his hand over father's nose to confirm whether he still breathed before he handed Baba the money. His face went blank when he saw Ade observing father's pulses.

"If any of you want to witness the sacrifice, follow me, please," the diviner said

"No, Baba," I said, not wanting a part in this. "That is not necessary."

Baba's eyes narrowed. "I do not advise faint hearts to witness it either, unless I am doing it directly on their behalf. Return by noon then."

I had no objection. It was best we returned when he was done.

Although, Mike remained suspicious and wanted to stick around to see if he was serious about the human sacrifice thing, Ade convinced him to leave. We did not go far, but settled in a local beer parlour in the same town.

By 12:00 p.m., the road shimmered in the midday heat and created a mirage. We drove through the express road, none of us dared to speak, marinating in tension that spiked as we arrived Baba's hut.

Unsure what I would find in his hut, doubts clouded me. This man might be a fake and father may already be dead. I did not trust his capability, and had followed along under Ade's recommendation. Since I convinced Mike into this, I couldn't back out. My heart slowed.

But I saw father seated on a wooden chair in front of the hut, and all my depression flew through the window.

Father was alive. He still had some herbs and feather mixture on his leg, face and hands but nothing beats the moment I saw him smile at us.

"Oh, Father." Mike broke down and wailed like a child.

I ran over and knelt beside father and hugged him so tight I feared he might suffocate.

Ade went over to have a chit-chat with Baba. They spoke in Yoruba dialect I didn't understand, but I watched them from where I knelt with father, and their gestures got me worried.

"Is everything okay over there, Ade?" I walked up to them.

"All is fine, sweetheart. I was just thanking Baba for his work."

I smiled at the Diviner thanking him with my eyes, he smiled back calmly, then I dragged Ade by his arm to the spot my father sat.

"Father, this isn't the best time for an introduction, but meet Adebayo, my boy-friend." I linked my hand through the crook of Ade's arm, and leaned my head on his chest. "Ade, this is my birthfather, Mr. Peterson."

They shook hands.

"Guys, loosen up a bit." I slammed their hands with mine to discontinue the long handshake, and they both burst into laughter.

"Time to go, Father," Mike cut in and held father's arm, helping him to the car. He gently slid him into the back seat and we all hopped in and drove off.

CHAPTER 26

We boarded a local flight to mother's place in Uyo with the exception of Ade. He stayed behind in Lagos for his work. With the excitement of having my complete family, I did not feel his absence so much. This was the first time I would live with my birthparents and brother under one roof.

Tears ran down my cheeks, happiness swelled inside me at the echoes of laughter from everyone. I was experiencing my childhood wrapped in just one moment. An inexplicable feeling, a sense of belonging and connection that made perfect meaning of 'blood is thicker than water'.

We sat at mother's living room recounting moments and laughing at ourselves, but reality set in sooner than expected when mother requested the details of what transpired.

No one spoke and the silence heightened mother's anxiety. Unable to keep a sealed lip any longer, I told her what I could.

"Jesus Christ!" She clapped a hand over her mouth. Tears ran down her cheeks as though a dam broke. "A human sacrifice?" Her voice rose. "None will carry blood on their hands into my house. I will not rebuild my family on sin. Tomorrow, everyone will come with me to see Pastor Akpan. We will pray for God's forgiveness and confess our sins. Then, we can stay as a family."

Silence.

Then father said, "We will do as you said. No need to get yourself worked up and ruin this moment."

But Mike was far from such co-operation, he shifted his weight to one leg.

"Sorry to disappoint everyone, but I will not meet any damn pastor. I am leaving." Mike stormed out.

The front door banged close behind him and mother broke into tears. This was not the way I expected the reunion to go.

"Please, do not do this to yourself. Father and I accepted to go with you," I said, but she was too heartbroken to hear me.

It took father and his antics to calm mother. Unable to stand her tears, I ran after Mike to speak some sense into him but he sounded cross and I left him. At least father agreed to come with us.

The following day, the three of us met with Pastor Akpan at his church. He asked us to confess our sin, so that God can grant us salvation. After the prayers, we rededicated our lives to Christ.

It was a surprise that father was willing to go through all.

We returned home, and I stayed a few more weeks with my birthparents before I prepared to visit Ade in Lagos.

"I will travel to my foster family in the U.S. from there," I told them.

They knew they would forever share me with the people who cared for me. I also called Ade and informed him of my decision. I was pleased with how my birthparents supported me but more gratified with

Ade.

When we spoke over the phone, he sounded ecstatic. "I can not wait to see you, sweetheart. I will pick you up at the airport," he said.

I had missed him those few weeks with my birthparents. As soon as I was done with my preparations, I took the next flight to Lagos.

Ade was waiting as I walked out of the arrival hall.

"How was your flight?" He pulled me into a hug.

"Beautiful." I kissed him long and hard. It felt as though I had not seen him in years.

We drove to a Japanese restaurant at Victoria Island with a cozy interior, sat at a table for two and reached for the menu. My eyes ticked right on rice and miso cooked in broth, and that was my order. Mike ate sushi and vegetables cooked in broth.

"This is delicious," he said and swallowed the last sushi wrap on his plate.

I sat back in my chair to watch him. "My miso was wow," I said. "I always have a nice time with you, Ade."

"Wait until you see what I planned for dessert." He winked.

"You know I can't just wait," I giggled. My eyes scanned his entire body. I bit the side of my lips and smiled.

He held my hands like a queen and led me off the table after he had settled the bills. He led me to the car, opened the front door, and bowed as I slid into my seat. We drove towards his apartment.

He blasted his horn and the security man opened the gate for us to drive through. Ade parked in front of the house and turned off the ignition.

He leaned over to the passenger's seat and whispered, "Put this over your eyes and give me your hand."

I looked at the piece of black cloth he held out to me, and then gazed doubtingly at him. "Ade, what are you up to?"

He grinned and held my hand. "Trust me on this, sweetheart."

"Okay, I t-rust you"

I wore the blindfold and let him lead me out of the car and into his house, hands in front of me, groping the air.

"Take the blindfold off and open your eyes," his voice guided me.

We stood in sitting room. I did not hear him open the door that let us in, or maybe it was already open, awaiting our arrival.

I blinked at the brightness of the chandeliers and the sight of my name spelt with heaps of white rose petals at the centre rug. A huge teddy bear stood next to the letters, a signage hanging on it's neck carried the words, WILL YOU MARRY ME?

Happiness simmered inside me.

Ade went down on a knee, in his hand was an open box with a ring in the middle.

"Will you spend the rest of your life with me, Grace?"

I never expected a proposal this evening,.

"Yes, oh yes, I will marry you, Mr. Adebayo." I stretched my hand and held my breath as he slid the ring in my middle finger.

"I love you, Mrs. Adebayo." He lowered his head and kissed the ring.

"I love you too, Ade." I helped him to rise.

Sparks became heated sensation and we made passionate love till the early hours of dawn.

The next day, actuality of the engagement made my heart skid. I couldn't wait for morning over in the U.S. to inform my family of my latest status. I was engaged to the man of my dreams, but the thought of Mike's reaction to the news lingered.

I picked my phone and dialled his number.

"Hello, kid sister."

The salutation startled me. He had never called me 'kid sister'.

I cleared my throat. "Mike! I have wonderful news."

"Yes, you do," he sounded excited.

"You sound happy, Mike." Something was up. "What's going on and where are you?"

"Bliss, I cannot wait to introduce Lisa to you. I am so in love." He whooped.

I needed a little time to absorb what I just heard. "Wait a minute. You found your soul-mate?"

"Met her in a flight. I am in Paris for a vacation." He giggled as though he had done something naughty. "I cannot wait for you to meet her, and also introduce her to Mum and Dad. They will freak out. She is so beautiful and half-black like us. Her Dad is a Nigerian, her Mum is British. She spent most of her life in the U.K. She-"

"Congratulations, Mike," I interrupted. He was saying too much all at once.

"Thank you, sister." He recollected himself and realized I must have called him for something. "Now what was your wonderful news?"

My news did not seem so wonderful anymore. He had soured my mood with his announcement. "I just got engaged."

"Wow! Was it Mike?" He kidded.

"Who else?" I rose to his dare.

And we laughed.

"I am still in Nigeria but will return to the U.S. in two days. When will you be back? I will love to meet Lisa," I said, a feeling of dread creeping up on me.

"In a month or less. Enough time to finish her work here in Paris. She will walk in the coming Paris fashion week this year."

"A Model. What a catch, Mike." I forced a cheer in my voice that I did not feel.

He chuckled. "Let me call you back when I am free."

"Okay." I frowned. She occupied him so much he could barely hold a phone call with me.

"Take care of you." He went off the line.

I took a deep breath. At least, he will leave me alone. I beamed at the thought of Ade and how wild we were in bed the previous night. I went in search of him. Maybe we could continue from where we stopped.

I found him in the room and we explore each others body, like fire and ice.

We painted each other with the colour of love for two more days till I had my fill.

I could be naughty when with someone as charming as Ade. I had to leave him for now to U.S. to see my foster parents, just the thing I wish I would not have to do. As I packed for the trip, I envisaged being Mrs Adebayo and always in his arms.

Back in the U.S., I broke my engagement news to my foster family. Their happiness showed in their moods, though Kennedy was the happiest. He analysed a grand wedding and painted me a mental picture.

"You are such a big dreamer, Kennedy. Your perception is always bigger than life." I laughed at the bogus, out of the ordinary, gipsy wedding he described

My parody did not stop him. He went on with his narratives, looking all serious.

My soul cheered when I saw my son hopping on his tiny legs. "Mummy is getting married to Daddy soon."

Hearing him repeat that slogan made my heart sink a bit. Soon another man would father my son. My stomach cramped, I wondered if Ade was good enough to father my son. It was no more about what I felt for Ade. I needed to think about my son and that got me scared. Both of them had no time to be together, to get to know each other.

I would discuss it with Mike when we meet, his views about having Ade in our son's life.

CHAPTER 27

Mike brought his girlfriend over to Nigeria at last.

I went over to his house to catch a glimpse of this mystery woman, who floored my brother and had him eating out of her hands.

"Lisa, meet my only sister, Blissful." He beamed, proud to show us off to each other. "Bliss, this is my love, Lisa."

"Nice to finally meet you, Lisa." I gave the model a hug. "Mike has raved so much about you."

"Same here, dear," she said coolly.

I found her too assured, too confident about her place in my brother's life.

"Will you excuse us, Mike? I will love to have a chit-chat with her alone."

Mike gave me a sharp look. "Will that be okay with you, sweetie?" he asked her.

I seethed inside. He needed her permission to leave. Next thing, he will need her permission to breathe.

"Yes, honey." She looked unbothered . "Allow us sometime together." Lisa smiled.

I studied her as we both waited for Mike to get out of earshot. Beautiful, with one of the best ivory skin I had seen, Lisa might be in her early 20s. She had a lovely British accent but I wanted to figure out what she hid behind those watchful blue eyes.

We chatted in the living room on the intricate of Lisa's life. In the space of an hour, I discovered she was not only a model, but also a self–described witch. She did not try to hide it.

"I was raised by a witch," she announced proudly. "My mother is a good witch. I believe my spell attracted Mike, and that confirmed he was my soul-mate."

Alarm bells chimed in my head. I was not sure I heard correctly that she used a spell on Mike. I fired the questions as they popped in my head.

"Does Mike know who you are?"

She inclined her head. "Yes. We both have no secrets from each other. He told me about his dark side and how he was raised. We, witches, don't harm others with our powers." Her smile got weird as she spoke.

I played it cool until I could understand her game.

"Welcome to the family." I held her hand and tried to keep calm as I led her to Mike. He stood by the window, catching a view of his garden and sipping brandy.

"I will take my leave now. I wish I could stay longer with you, Lisa, at least to continue our interesting discussion," I lied through my teeth, wishing to get as far away from her as possible. "How long will you be here with Mike?"

"I am leaving tomorrow morning unfortunately. I stopped over to meet you." She smiled in a way that showed she was glad I was leaving as well.

One thing was sure, confident in her spell, she came prepared for whoever intended to stand in the way of getting my brother as her man.

I needed support to tackle this challenge. I would wait for the appropriate time to tell Ade my truth about her. But I had so much on my plate, I should be preparing for my marriage and not worry about Mike and Lisa, and so should Ade.

I waved the pretty witch to the corner of my mind and focused on the task of planning a wedding in just few months.

CHAPTER 28

My marriage preparations kicked off before I could catch my breath. The activities buzzed in a whirl. We chose August of the same year we got engaged. That was a special month for Ade's family as they all shared the same birth month.

To be visibly present in all the meetings, I shuttled from U.S. to Nigeria, and so did Mike. Most meetings were fixed only for the immediate family members but he brought Lisa along. So far, she was the last person I wanted around, and her presence got on my nerves and lowered my vibes.

Mike never hinted me or anyone he would bring her along. And at the sight of her stepping out of his car, my jaw dropped and almost touched the floor. It made no sense having her tag along for such intimate family meetings. I tried not to make an issue out of it. My dislike of her doubled and I faked a smile.

"Hey, Lisa." I walked up to her.

"Hello, Bliss." She waved in her sophisticated way, weighing me. Her eyes sizing me up.

We hugged.

"I brought Lisa along. I hope you do not mind." Mike patted my back.

"What guts," I mumbled under my breath, mad that he would spring her on me and expect me to act cool. I could feel the fury burn in my eyes. I was not sure what was working me up, her presence or that she glued her witch-self to Mike.

"Hello, Bliss." Mike's voice snapped me out of my thoughts. He had this look on his face as though he found my reservations about his girlfriend amusing.

"Welcome to our home, Lisa." I acted the gracious host, and felt like biting my tongue.

"Thank you, Blissful," she replied graciously as if she had no clue of how much I disliked her.

Mike curved his elbow. She slipped her hand through the loop, and they both stepped past me. She cat-walked, confident, and smiled as they entered the house, leaving me to follow behind. She was sending an indirect message; she didn't need my approval to take her place in our home.

They stepped in to the living room majestically.

The shocked expression on my birthparents' faces gave me joy. It spelt what Mike and Lisa will get-nothing good at all.

"Good morning, sir and ma'am," Lisa greeted, unfazed.

"Good morning, young lady," both my parents chorused without enthusiasm.

I chuckled silently. Let the games begin.

Mike took the reins to break the uncomfortable silence. "Dad, Mum, I apologise for not informing you about bringing a guest over. I wanted to surprise everyone."

"And you have done just that, Mike," father joked. "We are surprised,"

"Have a seat, dear" Mother pointed to a chair beside her. She did not want to seem overly rude.

Lisa sat at the edge of the seat offered and crossed her legs. "Thank you, ma'am."

Nothing bothered her, not the coolness towards her. It made her more dangerous to me.

"She is Lisa, my friend, half-Nigerian too and a model," Mike announced proudly.

"You are welcome, Lisa." Father beamed, leaning forward in his chair. "Which of your parents is Nigerian?"

"My father is from Cross River State, Calabar. My mother is British. Mum said they met during their school days when Dad came to the United Kingdom to study." Lisa swung a leg, relaxed, pleased to be the centre of attention.

"Calabar is just here." Mother pointed to the door as if she meant the next building. "What can we offer you to drink? Grace, please get her some refreshment."

I got thrown sometimes hearing mother call me by the name she gave me at birth. But what threw me more was serving that thing hanging next to my brother. Seeing my hesitation, mother looked at me with eyes that almost pierced through my skin. She sometimes communicated with her eyes, especially when she knew I was not on the same page with her on a subject.

I dragged my feet over to Lisa's corner and whispered to know her preferred brand.

"Whatever you offer is fine." She dismissed me like a waiter.

I was close enough to slap her, instead I clenched my fist. The scent of her perfume hit me. I could not figure which designer she wore or whether it was her concocted spell. I went off to get a bottle of wine and wine glasses. I also brought plates of dry-meat and dipping sauce for everyone. Mike helped pour the wine.

I enjoyed my goat *suya*, which tasted sweeter as I listened to mother interrogate Lisa. I longed for drama, knowing mother's stand when it came to religion and belief.

Jovial, poise, Lisa gave answers back to back. Then I saw she would not bend easily as I presumed. There would be no drama tonight. I excused Mike to have a word with him in private.

"I will be right back, sweetie," he said to Lisa.

Lisa nodded, and he followed me to the room. Permission granted, I guessed. We had barely entered the study room before I turned on him, arms crossed over my chest, waiting for him to explain what the hell was going on.

"What is it, Bliss?" He leaned against the reading table, looking all eager to leave.

"Did she tell you she is a witch, Mike? Mother will not accept her if she finds out. Is this relationship even normal or some magick and you are caught in her spell? Are you sure, you-"

"I know her enough." Mike cut in. His nostrils flared. "Bliss, please, just be happy for me as I have been for you. What we had was incest. Now I am in love with Lisa, and it is eating you up, despite that you are getting married soon."

I needed Mike on my side on this.

"Calm down, Mike. This isn't about what we had, this is about family. I am looking out for my brother's happiness. Look at what father put us through because he got himself entangled with an occult group. Look at our son, Little Mike, the product of all the twist."

Mike was not having any of it. "You are as self-centred as Mother, Bliss. You never care about what makes me happy." He stormed out of the room and banged the door behind him.

I leaned against the wall to keep myself from falling. Maybe it was best to bury the topic and just be happy for him. Mike was old enough to make his decisions and choices. I returned to the sitting room determined to mind my business and not get involved any longer.

I sat beside father and observed the questions and answers that flew between Lisa and mother. It was unbelievable that they were both still at it.

"Did you say you are neither a Christian nor a Muslim?" Mother's eyebrows rose. "What are you, a Buddhist or Atheist?" Mother clasped her fingers to suppress her displeasure.

I sat up, certain that mother may not be able to withstand her reply.

"I am a witch, ma. We are good witches, my mother and I"

Mother's eyes almost bulged out of their sockets. "A witch?" She gulped, opened her mouth to say something, changed her mind and asked instead, "Have you ever visited your father in Cross River State?"

"Yes, ma." Lisa grinned, enjoying mother's shock. She was getting a kick from seeing mother worked up.

"And the people there know you are a witch?"

"No, ma. I only stayed for a couple of days. That was my first visit, so I didn't say much about myself. Besides, my father has another family there, and his wife didn't welcome me."

Mother exhaled her disappointment. "Here in Nigeria, witches are burnt alive." She sounded as though she would have preferred Lisa was burnt, than crossing path with her son.

"Mother! Please, stop," Mike cut in.

"It is okay, Mike," Lisa said. "Your mother is right. That does happen in Nigeria."

"Nothing wrong in being a good witch." Father tried to ease the tension. He squeezed mother's thigh to get her to relax. "My grandmother, Lady Methuen, led a coven of fourteen good witches. My mother, Sarah, was among the ladies and practiced magick even as a child. My sister, Dorothy, later joined them, but my brother and I did not. Back then, we disliked magick, spell casting and dancing ritual.'

Lisa giggled. She was either glad to have found a supporter, or that mother had a challenger. She struck me as someone who thrived on drama.

Father smiled and continued, "I still don't like dancing, but good witches are passionate people. They are free-spirited but compassionate. I think you have made a nice choice of a friend, Mike." He gave Mike a thumbs up.

Mother looked as though she had drunk a good dose of bitter-leaf juice. She was not Lisa's fan neither did she want her in the family. She would have loved to cover father's mouth with her palm. Her eyes tried to shut him up.

"Thank you, Father, you always say the truth," Mike teased and kissed Lisa's fore-head as if apologizing for mother's attitude.

Mother and I watched the duo in stony silence. I could not believe my paternal grandmother and aunt were witches. I shuddered, grateful to be marrying out of this family. I wiped sweat off my forehead and, when I realised Lisa's eyes never left my face, I smiled.

Father's revelation was a cold, embarrassing slap to mother. She felt guilt, and went over to mend fences.

"I am so sorry, Lisa, if I made you feel judged in anyway. I will love for us to get to know ourselves better. Stay at the guest house tonight, and let us talk over breakfast tomorrow. Goodnight." She walked off to her room.

I froze in my seat. They would sleepover at the same guest quarters with me. Steam vapourised from my ears and nostrils. Hopefully, their stay would be just for a night.

I made an invisible sign of the cross in the air.

That night, although I knew Lisa would flaunt some magick invocations, what happened took sleep out of my eyes.

In the room next to mine, Lisa and Mike made horrid chirpy, whinny sounds like wild animals on a sex marathon. I lay on my bed, staring at the ceiling, restless. The sound worsened. It became unbearable, endless. I ran into the bathroom but the shriek echoed in every corner of the quarters.

It didn't sound like love making between couples. More like sex with their transformed souls, bonding in the paranormal. That might explain why she called him her soulmate. The sound was beastly, evil.

I sweated, even with the air-conditioner on full blast, more afraid for Mike now. "I will never allow this beast marry my brother. I will ensure her fantasies faded before they began." I promised myself.

It was almost morning. I pressed my pillow over both ears and folded myself to a fetal position, knees tucked to my chin. When the noise diminished, I pondered from Ade to my son, Little Mike, to the late Pa iEhiosu and back to Ade.

"Too many secrets in this household," I exhale, "and I knew nothing about Ade's family, their dark secrets." I had many unasked questions. I had to know everything about his family, even the tiniest of his family history.

I was done with shocks, especially with what revealed itself, father's mother and sisters were witches and the entire family just heard of this because of Lisa.

God, do not let the family I am marrying into live on lies, and dark secrets like mine, please, I prayed.

CHAPTER 29

Troubled about what I might find with the Adebayos, I was tense when I returned to Lagos to be with Ade. I forced my smiles but he knew me too well to be fooled. Having endured enough of my moods, Ade pulled out a stool and sat facing me, sad. He worried about me.

"Sweetheart, you have been uptight since you returned," he said. "I thought it was a mood swing, but it has not worn off with time. We should be making plans for our traditional marriage."

I found his worrying touching, but at the same time a bit too much.

I held his shoulders, felt his muscles move under my palms. "Ade, the truth is, I know so little about your history. You promised a visit to see your grandparents, but we never got around to it due to your work. I do not want a repeat of what my family is going through right now. Maybe we are moving too fast."

A frightened look crossed his eyes. He was scared of losing me. "Ask anything you want to know, sweetie."

He wrapped his arms around my waist and lifted me. The scent of his masculine cologne and mint fresh breath brushed my nostrils, tempting me to kiss his succulent lips, but I wanted answers.

"Ade, do you belong to a secret society or occult kingdom? Do your parents belong to any?"

My question staggered him. He lowered me into a chair. "Grace, I am a Christian but, as a Yoruba, I also believe in our ancestors and deities. I do not belong to any society, secret or open, aside the Medical Society of Nigeria." He smiled "My parents do not belong to any occult, as far as I know."

I pushed harder. "The event that transpired at Mike's house got me worried. Why did you travel along with that powder substance, and what was that?"

He lifted my chin so that our eyes met. "I just told you I believe in my ancestors. I am a traditionalist. Most Yorubas go with a little of their deity everywhere, Grace."

"So what about that Baba?" I let him wipe the tears on my cheeks with a handkerchief.

"Grace, you have to trust me when I say nothing evil will befall you, little Mike or our unborn kids. We can postpone the marriage till you are ready, sweetie."

I hugged him tight. Fears of the unknown had weakened my trust in his love for me. He did not deserve to be punished for the sins of my father.

"It is okay, Ade. I trust you. Let us continue with the marriage plans."

His face lit up like a child with candy. He kissed me and I wrapped my arms around his neck.

"I don't want to hurt you, Grace," he mumbled.

"I agree, Ade. I wouldn't want you hurting me either." I bit my lower lip. "You said you did not belong to a secret group that could harm my son and I, now you are afraid of hurting me?' Tell me, Ade, how does those two tally?"

He stood, a smile tugging at his lips. "My Queen, I want the best for us, that is all I am saying. Na Naija blood make my English no smooth," he teased, covering his tracks with the Nigerian pidgin English.

We hugged and my body clenched. Flashes of our last sex slid in my head; on top the washing machine and his head buried between my legs, licking me clean down there.

I unbuttoned his shirt, kissed his nipples, and ran my tongue over the hairs around it.

"You have a masters in seduction, sweetie," he moaned. His hands played with my nipples which hardened under his touch.

"Don't stop," I groaned and squeezed his butt like I was juicing an orange.

He bit my nipple and sweet pains rocked my body.

"I like that," I mumbled.

"Really?" He lifted my skirt, buried his head underneath, and pulled my panties with his mouth. "How do you want it, darling?" he whispered in that deep baritone that melted all of me.

I wanted him there and then. "A quickie, honey. Give it to me right now.'

He slid his hardness inside me and hot liquid ran down my legs. He thrust, hitting fast as he whispered in my ears, "You are so sweet."

I sucked in my virginal muscles, holding off from cumming. Changing position, I knelt so he entered from behind. He rubbed my G-spot, thrust gently, giving me a wow stimulation.

"Do you like it, honey?"

"You are hitting all the right places." I shivered with pleasure.

He fondled my clit with his fingers. I felt myself on the edge. A rush of something hot.

"I am cumin, honey."' I tried to squelch my screams.

"'Let us do it, my love." His hips jerked faster.

Our orgasm hit, shaking us to the tip of our toes. We collapsed and breathed softly in each other's ears.

"Do not move. I will be right back." Ade disentangled himself. He returned with a bottle of cold water. "Sip, honey."

I took the bottle and gulped. I passed it back to him. He sipped and tossed the bottle aside. Then he spread my legs and sucked me clean until hot tears rolled down my chin.

"You are mine," I moaned. "Come over here, my master."

I dragged down his pants and took his erect penis in my hands, ran my tongue over the tip, all the way down, licking down to his balls. When his legs trembled, I throat up his penis, swallowing him inch by inch. He moaned and cried out my name.

"Yes, darling," I answered and sucked his balls, loving how he screamed in ecstasy. I held his gaze and commanded him meekly but as a boss lady. "Cum for me, master."

He splashed all over my face.

"I am so sorry, honey." He smiled.

"Clean it up, master." I laughed.

He left and returned with a damp towel. He wiped my face, and then kissed my forehead.

"Let me get warm water ready so I give you a bath, honey," he said and dashed into the bathroom.

After our warm bath, he taught me how to prepare his favourite Yoruba soup, *Ofe Riro*, a Nigerian Spinach Stew, teasing me as he gave directives on steps to follow.

CHAPTER 30

Time flew when a date is fixed.

My introduction came in a blink and my foster family flew in from the state. My birthparents and Mike, all convened in Grandmother's place in Benin. The females wore the Bomba dresses made as tunics, while the men wore long boubou stylish cotton shirt over a pair of trousers.

Ade's family had the men in their Yoruba Apada, while the women flashed lace *wrappers* with matching lace blouse tops. Drop-dead handsome, in his light blue Apada and a dressing shoes, Ade killed his native outfit more than his English attires.

Still caught up admiring Ade, I was snapped out with a, "Greet your soon-to-be in-laws and husband, and then leave the hall until we send for you," Pa' Obaseki said.

The introduction ceremony had started, an indoor occasion meant for immediate family members. A table at the centre partitioned the living room in two. My family sat on the right, Ade's family occupied the left. Drinks stacked up on the table alongside glasses and voices spoke in loud tones with laughter in-between.

I remained in my room, imagining the activities out there until Pa called me back into the hall.

"Grace, this young man," he pointed to Ade, "brought his family to ask for your hand in marriage. Do you know him?" the spokesman asked.

I peeped at the guest from under my lashes. "Yes, sir. He is my friend."

The people mumbled amongst themselves.

"We have heard from you that he is not a stranger. Should we accept the Kola and drink they came with?"

"Yes, sir. Please, kindly accept them," I said.

He reached for the bottle of dry gin and a kola nut that Ade's father held out, and passed them to my birthfather.

"Thank you," my father said.

"Do you accept to marry the young man whose gifts we have received?" the spokesman asked me.

"Yes, sir. I do,"

Claps and cheers filled the room.

"You may go until we call you again." The spokesman turned aside to give Ade's family the marriage list.

"That is the same list my father was given when he came for mother's hand in marriage," Grandmother said. "It is so for every female family member."

Ade's people would buy the content on the list alongside the dowry they will present to my family. I couldn't see the listed items but heard voices of both family members arguing, disagreeing, and also agreeing. This went on for a while and then laughter followed. Food and drinks went round, including garden egg, kola, drinks and water. .

Towards the end of the ceremony, the spokesperson called me to bid the people farewell. Mother had told me that in the Benin culture, introduction ceremony was to enable both families meet officially. Collecting the marriage list meant mine was successful.

A few months later, the Adebayos returned as agreed. They brought the items on the list with them.

Ahead of their arrival, Ade called my line before dawn and urged me to prepare.

"I am coming to get my wife today, so get ready, sweetheart," he said.

Happiness streaked through me like a comet. It elevated my mood.

"Mother, they are returning with the items on the list today," I screamed.

"I know that, Grace. We are prepared to receive them," she said.

Soon both family members reconvened.

Spokesmen from both families confirmed the items. To make it easier, one of them read and the other brought the items out. They were focused on ensuring not a piece of kola nut was left out.

I felt sold at the sight of yam heaps, palm wine kegs, bags of rice. The bubbly joy disappeared and my disappointment surged as a few elders argued as if those items were all I was worth. Unable to endure my thoughts any more, I ran out of the hall. Grandmother came after me.

"Wait, Grace. She hurried to catch up.

I stopped and covered my mouth, sick to my stomach. Grandma hugged me, and the tears kept coming. I could not stop it.

"Grandma, I feel as if I am being sold. Was that all I am worth? Yams and rice?"

"Poor child." Grandma caressed my back. "This is tradition. I was married this way, same as your mother. Remember, you agreed to marry the Benin way, else you would have gone to America to do it your way. Besides, you are marrying into a prestigious Nigerian family. The Adebayos are well known for their philanthropies."

"But Grandma, I- I-I don't care about their social status. I feel like I am not ready or I am about to make a mistake.

"It takes most women a lot of time to accept they are getting married. It is the fear of starting a family, of the unknown." Her mouth twisted in a ghostly smile. "Do not worry. We are all here for you. Who sells a grandchild for some tubers of yam?" she asked in a comical voice. Her old face wrinkled in a smile.

We laughed. She wiped the tears off my face.

"We, women, have the capacity to face our fears without telling the world. Let's go back in. Behave yourself, all right?"

"Yes, ma." I nodded.

I watched Grandma return to the hall, her solito shoes slapping the sole of her feet with a clap. The words she told me ran through my head until she disappeared into the hall. I followed with a smile to my seat.

No one seemed to notice my earlier absence . I had missed out on a couple of activities. I came in to see that Ade's father knelt, Ade's hands on his father's shoulders.

"Ade!" Our spokesman called six times.

Ade remained silent.

I wanted to speak but Grandma shut me in.

"Shhhh, Grace," she whispered, "don't say a word. This is tradition."

Then the spokesman called the seventh time, "Adebayo."

Ade answered, "Yes."

The spokesman said, "Dr. Adebayo," he addressed Ade's father, "we are giving our daughter, Grace Peterson, to your family so you could take good care of her and not to maltreat. We will never take it kindly if she is maltreated."

Ade's father promised everyone they will take good care of me.

The spokesperson turned to me. "Your responsibility as a wife is to help Ade build a home."

I replied in the affirmative.

Then Ade and I were called to feed each other and seal the Occasion. We were given honey and bitter kola, a sweet and bitter significance. Both families celebrated for the rest of the evening.

Ade and I sneaked out to sit under the mango tree in the compound, near the fence. We discussed Mr. Fuoye, their spokesperson. He did a meticulous job interpreting every Yoruba dialect the elders spoke.

Another successful event done that pushed us nearer to the D-day, the traditional marriage, happening this Saturday.

CHAPTER 31

I woke up to the smoke and smell of burnt cow, aromas of traditional cuisines that made my stomach growl and hungry warms squirm. They were firm reminders that today is my day.

I jumped out of bed, peeped through the window at a small hut the women had built at the backyard. Cooking happened on an open fire-wood three-legged pot. The women hurried about, gossiping in-between. I craned my neck to see the other side of the compound. The men mounted canopies, and a few that already stood were decorated with the Benin traditional clothe material, little calabashes and beads.

I was still at the window when my birthmother and my foster mother walked in.

"Good morning, Grace."

"Congratulations, Bliss."

I turned around and smiled shyly as I returned to my bed. "Good morning, Mums."

"We came to say a prayer for you and also give our motherly blessings," my birthmother said.

Both women held my hands, one on each side, and poured their heart's blessings.

"God, we commit today into your hands," my birthmother said.

"Grant it with your presence," my foster-mother added.

"Amen," I said.

They were interrupted by my cousin, Ivie.

"Here she is." My cousin pointed at me.

A lady walked in with a small metal box. "I am Queeneth, a make-up artist. Your husband, Ade, hired me to give you a make-over."

"Welcome, Queeneth." I returned her smile.

"Excuse us then, Grace," Mum said and both women left the room.

Queeneth sew some beads into my hair to make it stand out. She called it *Eko-Okuku*, and attached a beaded crown, *okuku*, to make me appear taller. In her professional but friendly manner, she taught me the Edo tradition and what I should expect today.

She waited for me to bath and have my breakfast. Then she gave me a 'face beat'. I could not recognise my reflection in the mirror. My dress accentuated my curves and complemented my beaded cape, Ivie obo, coral beads on both hands, a beaded earring and a beaded clutch to match. I looked like a goodness.

Cameras flashed. The videographer's light fixed on my face. All I heard for the next few minutes was "Smile, face the camera, sit upright, this way, please. Yes, one more." The camera men directed me until the celebration kicked off outside with loud traditional music that filtered into my room. The Master of Ceremony stole the day with a humour that had the people rolling in stitches.

My son walked in, cute in his traditional attire. "Mummy, you look so beautiful," he said.

I kissed his soft cheek, staining it with my red lipstick. "Oh, sorry honey." I wiped the outline of my lips off his cheek.

"Don't clean it, Mummy. I love my new face tattoo." He touched his cheek.

"All right, honey. But let me wipe this one off and do another for you after the occasion, okay?" I teased.

"All right, Mummy."

I pulled out a wipe and dabbed his cheek. Kennedy walked in with two glasses of wine,

"Congratulations, sis." He handed a glass to me. "You look beautiful." He fingered my beads.

"Thanks, Ken."

"Let me take little Mike along, so you can do your thing," he said. "Come on, little man, let us go." He held out his hand and both of them walked out of the room.

I purse my lips. None of my fathers had come to see me. I left the bed and went down the corridor in search of them. My fitted dress restrained my steps. Lisa's voice behind one of the doors made me stop. I leaned forward, trying to pick out her words.

"I have to let my sister know what she is getting herself into," Mike's voice echoed.

"That is not a good idea. It is better she doesn't know. I believe if it was okay for her to know, Adebayo would have told her everything."

"But why keep such a secret from his own wife? I told you everything the day we met, didn't I?"

"And that was why we clicked from the beginning. We are more than lovers, we are soul-mate but I don't see them connecting beyond the love sparks. Love is never enough, you know?"

"Lisa, dear! She still has a choice now. I have to protect my sister."

"No. I will make a charm bracelet to protect her for now. Is that okay?".

A little hesitation. "That is fine!"

———

I tried to sneak back to my room, but my feet thudded against the door frame.

I walked fast, my throat dry, my palms moistened. I wiped both hands on my dress, shattered by what I heard.

Seconds later, Lisa walked in. My heart lurched. Mike had brought this witch here and maybe she had brought her so called charm bracelet with her.

"Hey, pretty bride." She smiled, oozing confidence.

"Hey, Lisa and Mike."

"Congratulations," they chorused as though they had practiced the routine.

"What is she doing here?" I asked before I could stop myself.

"I brought you some good luck charm bracelet, to keep away evil eyes from you today," Lisa said. She brought out a blue-eye pearl bracelet from her designers clutch, and held it out to me.

"Oh, really. That is so kind of you, Lisa." I could not keep the disgust from my voice. I did not collect the gift.

"Take it, Bliss. She means well for you. Days like this often come with good and evil," Mike said.

"No, thanks. But I appreciate the thoughtfulness." I faked a smile.

"It is okay, Bliss. We wish you all the best today. Enjoy your day," Lisa said and dragged Mike by the arms and out of the room, just before the medians came singing and dancing.

"We are here to dance you out to your husband," one of them said.

"All right but I am not a good dancer," I warned.

"It is okay. No matter how you dance, you are beautiful and remain today's focus."

We danced out, with me in-between the two medians in the front row. I waved my hands and wiggled my waist. The crowd kept cheering as we danced to greet the guests.

The MC directed me to my spot. He called out Mike and both my parents to where I stood facing the crowd. Ade and his parents were called to stand at the MC's left. The MC took my hand and placed it in my birthfather's palm. He asked my foster father to join hands, and they both gave me over to Ade before the cheering crowd.

Pa Obaseki blessed our union, and the MC invited sir Waziri Oshiomah, a famous Edo singer on stage. Both families danced. Some flopped in the struggled to move to the juju beat, while others got their groove on. Pastor Akpan came to congratulate us. Dignities followed suit, spraying naria notes, dollars, pounds in the air.

I overheard a conversation between my birth mother and pastor Akpan. They were shouting, trying to be heard above the sound of the instruments.

"There are people walking on air, whose feet do not touch the ground amongst us. I tried to figure who they are or who brought them, but all I saw was snake-like creatures and giant scorpions. They are evil. Please, keep an eye on your daughter," Pastor Akpan said

Mother noticed my presence. She smiled and nodded.

I danced towards father to let him in on what I heard, but met him talking with Ade's father, in company of some affluent-looking men.

"Why did you invite them here? I never knew you were one of them, Adebayo," father sounded cross.

"Neither did I know you were one of the Angels, Peterson." His tone deepened. "We are here for our children. Let us keep it that way for today. Is that all right with you?" Dr Adebayo asked.

Father saw me and lowered his voice. "All right then." He left them and danced towards me. "Congrats, honey. Where is your husband?"

I shuttered. "What is going on, please?"

"Grace, do not let unnecessary cares ruin your day." He looked around and spotted Ade dancing with my foster parents. He moved me stylishly to Ade.

"Adebayo, dance with your wife, will you?" He handed me over to him and walked away.

"Ade, we need to talk," I began, but a voice interrupted.

"Here they are. The latest couple in town," my foster mother said.

The families surrounded us. My son, little Mike, was not let out. He and Ken displayed their rehearsed choreographed dance moves, lightening my mood from the growing dread since I overheard Lisa and Mike's conversation.

Time to cut the cake, then food, drinks and water went round the tables. Cameras flashed, soft music lingered in the background. I looked around and spotted the local news van. The television news reporter had a mic and was interviewing my parents. Then I saw Lisa and Mike heading out to also grant their interview. Adrenaline pumped through my body, I wanted to head over there and stop that interview but the MC's voice interrupted.

"Let's welcome the latest couple, Mr. and Mrs. Adebayo."

Amidst the hails and claps, Ade walked me forward. Panic seized me. What I dreaded had befallen me. There were dark secrets in the Adebayo's family just like mine. The traditional marriage just ended but my reality stared me in the face.

Everyone packed up to leave. Only Ade and I were left to start our lives as a couple. I was Mrs. Adebayo now and my husband was my new future, so I cleaved to him like glue. We drove to Govict Hotel and Suites, where Ade had lodged the night before.

Silence reigned in the car, both of us with millions of things to say but unsure where to start. The marriage was a mistake. I couldn't wait to get to the room and talk to him about it.

"Did you enjoy our marriage ceremony today, my wife?" Ade broke the ice.

"Partly."

"What happened to the rest of it?" he reached over to hold my hand.

"Demons showed up. Ade, do you know your father belongs to some group or occult society? It looks like either my birthfather and he belongs to the same society, or he knows where your father belonged." I narrated all I observed.

Ade exhaled. "Honey, you worry so much. We sorted this topic earlier. Today marks the beginning of our lives together. Let us not start on a rough note." His voice sounded strained, revealing he was at his limit.

The rest of the ride was quiet until we arrived at the hotel.

A surprise party awaited us as we drove in. His colleagues and friends had all gathered at the hotel.

Ade whispered. "I don't like your mood. Cheer up or fake a happy face. All my friends are here, so they would not misunderstand us." He kissed me and stepped out of the car, he walked to the passenger's side and opened the door.

"All hail the latest couple," Tunde shouted as we walked in.

Tunde was his best friend, who he picked to be the best man at our white wedding the following Saturday.

My cousins, Ihuanedo, and her sister, Ivie, alongside others came to hug and congratulate us. Lisa and Mike came over.

"Congrats again, guys,' Mike said and turned to introduce Lisa.

"Lisa!" Ade screamed.

"Ade!" Lisa smiled. "Congratulations."

They hugged.

I froze. Speechless. And so did Mike.

"How do you know each other? She stayed all her life in the U.K.," I mumbled.

"Sweetheart, Lisa is my maternal cousin. We only met once when she came searching for her biological father."

I echoed, "Your cousin?"

"Yes," Lisa chipped, "until I saw their banner at the venue, I didn't know it was our own Dr. Adebayo. I saw my father at the venue, but it wasn't the proper place to introduce my handsome." She swung Mike's hand as if she were a child.

The witch was part of my family with or without her married to my brother, Mike. My mood crashed again.

Ade whispered, "That expression, Grace."

I offered a sheepish smile. Grandma said women have the capacity to handle anything without letting the world know. I just did that now, Grandma, I hope you are proud of me. I tried to hold back the tears.

Ade disappeared with his friends and only remembered me when someone asked to know his new wife. He wrapped his hands around me.

I was watching a new Ade surface, not the same man that could barely see me part from his side. I cowered in the midst of my cousin, Ivie, and his brother.

CHAPTER 32

The white wedding rowed off at St. Peter's Catholic Church where the Adebayo's fellowshipped. A colourful reception followed with personalities in attendance and the State governor graced the occasion. My favourite musician, Tuface Idibia, performed his song 'African Queen' when we took to the dance floor.

I wanted the union to be different from what I experienced with Ade a few days after the traditional marriage. If God answered prayers, this was my heart cry. I was lost in thought throughout the reception, and did not realise it had almost ended until Ade's father handed us an envelope.

"Grace, here. Take this for your honeymoon. Make sure you guys leave immediately after the reception so you can catch your flights. You will get clothing there as well." He turned to his son. "Phone and let me know how long you will stay."

In the envelope were tickets to Dubai, his Business Expenses Card and a visa CTA hotel card.

Just like he said, we did not waste any time after the reception. We left directly from the hall to the airport, boarded our flight and off we went to Dubai.

My honey moon in Dubai involved a yacht tour. We cruised out in the water for some alone time to the Dubai creek, surrounded by iconic landmarks and unparalleled beauty of the Arabian Gulf.

The city oozed glitz, glamour and excitement. We lodged at the iconic Burj Al Arab hotel and Ade displayed his dance moves at the sky view bar night club. I shopped at Dubai Mall for our clothes with Ade, and his love for adventure had us soaring up to the observation deck at the Burj Khalifa. We also explored the air-conditioned soak at Madinat Jumeirah. Dune-bashing and hot air balloon. those outdoors activities added a healthy dose of adventure to our experience.

We had romantic dinners at different restaurants but cousins at the gourmet were out of this world. We had it all; money to spend, time to waste, both of us for intimacy, but the moon in the honey didn't last long before the sun brought its insufferable heat that ended our stay prematurely.

It was our discussion that brought the heat.

"Ade, can we talk about our future?" I lay across his legs reading a novel.

"Okay, but come lay by my side instead," he said.

I was heavy on his legs.

I repositioned beside him, combing his hair with my fingers. "Ade, can we go live in America instead of Nigeria, please?" I gave him a puppy-eyed look.

"My answer will be no, sweetheart."

"Please, Ade, I don't think I will like it there in Nigeria, staying permanently. Our kids will be better in U.S."

He cut me off. "This is not even contestable. I will not leave my life, father's hospital and other businesses I run here, to start up in the U.S. because I married an American." He turned over and looked at me. "Why are you bringing this topic now, Grace?"

Tears gathered in my eyes. "'Honey, after what happened at our traditional marriage, I am not sure I . . . "

"You sound self-centred. Can you hear yourself? You, you, you. Kill that fear before it kills our marriage, girl." He grabbed his shirt and walked out of the hotel room.

We landed back in Nigeria the following day.

As newly married couples, we had to thank our families for their support during the marriage processes. My father in-law invited my biological parents over to his house. My foster family and my son, little Mike, had returned to the States before we got back from the trip. Ade's father hosted the little family thanksgiving party on behalf of Ade and I.

Ade prostrated to thank everyone. I knelt in the Yoruba's way of greeting elders. At the end of the little party, We left them to continue talking and retired inside. Mother and Ade's mum left the men to the room to have their women talk. Ade left me alone to God-knows-where.

I sat at the end of the dinning hall, admiring the awards that hung on the wall. I wowed at the Nigerian Healthcare Medical Awards and the prestigious Lasker Awards, an American Nobel award to a living person who made major contributions to medical science or who performed public service on behalf of medicine.

Ade's father must be a great man to have achieved all these, I thought. Then I heard something that chilled me.

"You must allow the dark shadow master take her soul if you want to be free."

"But she is my wife. I have put her through so much, Adebayo. You have no ideas what that woman suffered because of me, because of The Church Of The Angels."

"Pete, how could you say I have no idea? Do you know Ade's mother was taken by the dark shadows? My wife has no child and that is in exchange for who I am today. Ade is not her biological child. My first wife, Mmayen, was from Calabar, Cross River State."

One of the awards slipped from my hand and crashed on the tiled floor, interrupting them. I knelt to pick the broken pieces and tried to reconstruct it, when Ade's father walked in.

"Grace, hope it did not hurt you," he said.

"Sorry, sir. I was fascinated by all these awards and tried to read them."

"That is okay, dear. Call one of the aids to clean that up. Where is your husband?"

"Sir, he left . . . "

"Left you alone? Find him and come with him, please." He walked back to the meet my father in the sitting room.

Few hours later, Ade walked in with a friend.

"I am so sorry, sweetheart, I had to pick up Dr. Timothy from the airport." He kissed my cheek and made to walk pass, but I held his arm.

He turned with a hard look, noticed his friend's expression, and then mellowed.

"Yes, sweetheart?" He smiled.

"Your Dad asked that we see him when you return."

"Excuse us, Tim. Sit over there. I will be right back."

His friend gaped at us.

We walked in to find Ade's dad alone. I had no idea my parents left. I anticipated seeing my mother so I could hint her on what I knew about father.

"Dad, you asked for me," he said.

His Dad sounded annoyed. Either he knew I overheard them or because I was left alone.

"Junior, how dare you leave your new wife all alone without informing her on your movement? I do not want this to repeat itself. Take charge of your home."

I held Ade's hand tight.

"Yes, Dad," Ade said.

They spoke about the hospital and Ade left. We picked his friend Tim and drove him to Dolphin Estate. After we booked him in, we reversed to drive home. I decided to share what I heard.

"Honey, while I waited, I overheard your Dad and mine speak about the dark shadow. I think my mother might be in danger."

Ade flared. "Wait a minute, sweetheart, why will you not stop this before it turns into something else?"

"Ade, give me a chance to explain. I am your wife. I do not have any one else to talk to, please, hear me out."

"You accuse your father and mine. I can not believe this has degenerated to this level. Please, stop right now, sweetheart."

"How did your mother die? Mrs. .Mmayen Adebayo," I asked suddenly.

He jerked, almost losing control of the car.

"What are you talking about, Grace?" He pulled the car over by the road side and turned off the ignition. "Let this be your last of mentioning that name. She did not exist. The only Mrs. Adebayo is Mrs. Cecilia Adebayo and she is my mother. Is that clear?"

How could he deny his own mother even in death?

Terror coursed through my veins. I smelled something sinister, and figured it wise not to speak to Ade about these things. He might be one of them. I might be in danger.

"I am sorry, honey."

"Good." He hugged me, started the car and drove off.

I had to see my mother as soon as possible.

Few weeks later, I took permission from my husband to travel to Akwa Ibom to see my parents. He granted me two days. He had gone with his father on a business trip.

I told my mother everything about father's non-repentance, and unwillingness to leave the organisation.

"Be careful," she pleaded. "I will see pastor Akpan about all you have told me. I will ask your father myself." Her lips twisted. My birthmother could be fierce when stepped on.

"Mother, I think you should not ask him. Let us both be careful. Let us talk to Pastor Akpan first."

She changed the topic. "Your brother, Mike, still gallivants around town with that lady, Lisa. I don't know what to do to bring him to his right senses."

"Hmm, Mother, do you know Lisa is my husband's cousin?"

"When did you get to know this?"

"The night of my wedding."

"Good God." Tears rolled down her weak eyes, the last thing she ever wanted was to see me unhappy or struggle after marriage.

We prayed.

Mother was my best friend and confidant. I tried not to give father any negatives vibes. I was myself around him until I left to Lagos.

Back home, my husband and I tried to work out our marriage. The communication improved as long as his father or family was not mentioned. Everything went smoothly, until I received a call that shattered my peace.

"I know your little secrets. I will spill it to your husband if you and your mother dare stop my marriage."

"And what is my little secret?"

"Do not play dumb with me. Who is the father of your son, little Mike? And by the way, we are taking him from you once I marry your brother."

"You will never marry him."

The line went dead.

It was Lisa on the phone.

I sat on my bed, numb. I had to tell my husband about this myself. It wasn't a secret, just that we did not discuss it.

I dialled my husband's number. It rang. He might be in the operation room.

I sent a message: Honey, please, we need to talk. Call me or come home as soon as you can.

But before he got home, she already told him.

"Welcome, honey. How was work?"

"Hectic, sweetheart, I got the shock of my life today."

My heart hammered. "Did you see my message?"

He pulled off his cloth, tossed it in the laundry basket, and entered the bathroom. He sang in the shower, a habit when unhappy. That was his way of relieving negative energy.

"Sweetheart, is your brother your son's father?"

I was quiet. So this witch told him. She was trying to break my home.

"Yes, he is, but I did not know who he was then. Neither did he know we were siblings."

"Your brother, Kennedy, told me little Mike's father was dead."

"Kennedy and my foster parents do not know the truth. My son, too, does not know the truth."

"Yet you nagged me and my family about secret keeping? What a person you are, Grace."

That was the last normal discussion we had. From that day, everything went south. My life began to scramble before me. Mike threatened to take custody of our son. He did not like the idea of me leaving the child with my foster parents.

I tried talking to my husband about it.

"Let him have his son. Do not deny them of bonding, and stop lying to your son."

"You do not understand, Ade, I am-"

"Excuse me." He picked his car keys from the table. "See you when I return."

Tears welled as I dialled mother's number.

"Hello."

"Hello," it was father's voice instead. "Father, please, hand the phone over to mother."

"Your mother is ill. I am sorry, she cannot speak."

"What...what is wrong with her? Where is she?"

"She is at the specialist hospital here. She suffered a stroke."

"Oh, Father, why? Why did you allow them? She is all I have. I hate you, Father. I curse you. If anything happens to Mother, I will never forgive you."

"Grace, I did nothing. Why are you saying all this?"

I cut the call and wept for hours until I slept off on my bedroom floor.

My husband met me that way. He lifted me and unconsciously I said, "She is going to die. They will kill her."

"Sweetheart, who is she? You have not had your bath. What is happening to you, sweetheart?"

"My mother suffered a stroke. She is admitted at the hospital. Take me there, Ade please." I was losing it.

The following day, we took the first flight to Uyo, picked up pastor Akpan from his church, and drove to the hospital.

Mum could barely say a word or smile. Her face twisted to one side and drooled saliva.

"Oh, Mother." I wept. "See what they have done to you."

Pastor Akpan held me back, preventing me from speaking further.

"Let us pray," he said. "Father, your daughter has embraced you and your salvation. Please, may no darkness take her. May her soul return to you on the angel's wings. Thank you, Jesus."

What was he saying?

"Excuse me, Pastor," I turned to Ade. "Please, let me have a word with the pastor, honey."

Ade nodded, and we walked out of the hospital emergency room.

"Pastor, why didn't you cast out the devil tormenting my mother like you used to? Do you want her dead? What have you seen that made you pray that way, pastor?" I cried. "They have killed her. Oh, my God, have mercy."

"Grace, your mother will sleep when it is time. Do not weep, my daughter. She has fought a good fight of faith."

"Oh God." The word sleep hit me harder than a hammer on a nail. I ran back to the room. Mother was still not fully conscious.

"Hers is an acute stroke and the doctors are doing a great job," Ade said.

Just then, Father walked in with Mike. We were complete family, but I suspected all of them had a hand in this. Mike, father and Ade.

I was alone, Mother and I. A bitter reality that sparked my temper.

Mother did not make it.

My world crumbled. I went temporary insane with grief. I became depressed, isolated, withdrawn. As a doctor who understands mental health, Ade showed support, but most times he snapped at me.

"Why will everything be so hard with you?" Other times he would say, "You brought this upon yourself."

flashes of what father and Ade's father said that day played in my head. It tormented me. They took my mother from me.

My mother was buried at the cemetery, the worst day of my life. I could not bear seeing the coffin lowered. I charged at my father-in-law. who was dressed in a black suit and wore a look of innocence.

What was he and father doing here? To mock her in her grave?

"Evil man," I screamed at Ade's father, "you both killed her. Father, she loved you with all her being. Shame on you."

Ade and the others at the site held me back.

Everyone whispered as my husband forced me into the car and drove off without letting me witness the first soil drop on my mother's grave.

Molten anger rolled through my veins and poured out hate in my soul, I must find out all their hidden secrets and expose all of it, I swore to myself.

Sorrow overshadowed me and ate me up like a mote on a leave. My heart sought to revenge my mother's death. My husband thought I was depressed and sent me a psychotherapist.

CHAPTER 33

"I admire your courage, Mrs. Adebayo. This session is the first step to your healing. Allow me help you through this process."

I sat motionless. Ade felt that locking me in here and sending a psychotherapist would stop me from exposing them. But he lied to himself. I would avenge my mother's death.

"You are not alone. Share your pain with me. Why do you feel your father and father in-law are responsible for your mother's death?"

I shook my head. She might never understand. "You won't understand, please. Don't waste your time with me."

"Why do feel I will not understand? Is it some kind of mystery? Was it in your dreams? Was it all in your head? Is the little voice talking to you?"

The question sounded funny, I laughed. "You think I am crazy, right?"

"No, I think you are suffering a trauma and need this session to offload."

"You feel some cheap talk with you or few pills in a yellow container can heal me? Let me tell you something, it is hard to be normal when you are surrounded by abnormalities. See yourself out when you are done." I walked out on her and entered my room.

Ade barged into the room.

"Sweetheart, the therapist complained about your unwillingness to co-operate with her. Do you truly want this marriage to work? Please, tell me, Grace." He looked frustrated and tired. He must have had a rough day at work.

"I am fine, honey. All I need is that you listen and work with me." I walked over to him.

He strolled away as though my touch disgusted him.

This was a different side of Ade I never knew. How did I become his wife? How did things deteriorate this much?

I blacked out.

I woke up surprised to see Ade by my side.

"This is a clear symptom of Post Traumatic Stress Disorder PTSD. Have some pity on yourself, Grace," he said.

Pain gripped my body. I shivered like a rabbit. "You are tormenting me, Ade. Please, do not do this to me."

He waved my words away as if fanning gnats. "You either help yourself or I admit you in a psychiatric home. I will not let you ruin us."

Fear became substance. Mother told me to be wise.

"Okay, honey. I will see the Psychotherapist tomorrow." I smiled broad like a hyena.

He kissed my forehead and took me to get a bath.

The therapy sessions were lame. I got absolutely nothing out of them, just the stiff face of my therapist. In some sessions, I became the therapist and she the patient. I enjoyed seeing her shrug helplessly. Finally all was over. I handled it as a child and ghosted her, even when we both sat facing each other.

"Congratulations, Mrs. Adebayo. We have concluded our sessions successfully," she said.

"Let my husband know this," I requested.

"Sure." She smiled as if she just won a trophy. I could not wait for her to exit before shutting my door.

"Do you really think everyone needs therapy?" I grinned. "You are working for your money but, please, Mrs. therapist do not miss the part of informing my husband about our successful end." I giggled.

Triumphantly, Ade walked to me as he returned from work. "Sweetheart, I am so proud of you."

He carried me to the room and lay me gently on the bed. He pulled down my denim jeans and thrust into me. No foreplay, this wasn't lovemaking. This was him displaying his dominance over me. Our love making was always eruptions of passion, now all that was left was a few seconds of ejaculation.

I lay numb. Nothing left here for me to hold on to, except memories which might soon fade over time.

Where was the Ade, I used to rumple over, his body in mine? Hot tears rolled down my cheeks. I wiped them off and went to the sitting room to see some movies.

Later that day, Mike called to inform us of his wedding to Lisa. They tied the knot in the U.S. Lisa was now Mrs. Peterson. He did not even allow our mother's flesh to detach from her bones. Goose bumps broke all over my body. All of them now against me, darkness against the truth.

I had to be wise and smart. I must not allow them kill me like they did Mrs. Mmayen Adebayo and my mother. Calmness rolled in. My bubbling self hopped around the house, sampling my bad singing voice. I forced myself to be happy or appear so, in order to get

Ade to draw me closer, and that worked.

Ade took us for dinner at his parents'. A quiet occassion, only the eyes spoke as we ate and listened to the chattering of the cutleries.

After the dinner, I sneaked into Ade's mother room. The click of the lock drew her attention. The scowl on her face startled me, making my heart pound.

"Can I, please, speak with you, ma?"

She was my last hope in unraveling this madness. Her well-rounded bottom settled into a chair by her dressing mirror. She looked as though she saw a ghost, horrified was the right expression on her face.

"Let me hear you, young lady," she said.

"You are not Ade's biological mother, are you?" I asked.

Her spirit must have left her body momentarily. She squared her shoulders, and appeared lost for a second. Then she heaved her heavy frame out of the chair.

"Who told you that?"

"Ade did not tell me. I overheard a conversation between your husband and my father before my mother's death." My eyes singed with pains.

She looked pitifully at me and sighed. "I was as innocent as you when I married him. He fooled me into falling in love with him. He never truly loved me. I was a cover for his sins and a trophy for his reputation." She looked pissed. "I became Ade's mother instantly. His dead mother's name was a taboo to mention. I ran back home as all my kids either died after a few months or were still born." The tears fell. She smiled amidst her tears and mucus runny nose. "I have a daughter. I named her Cecilia as me. None of them know this. She is with my aunty in sokoto." She leaned towards the table to get a nose wipe.

I pushed the pack close to her and she blew her nose and continued with a stiff face.

"When I took in, I staged a quarrel and ran back to my aunt's. She hid me until I delivered, but I took ill to the point of death." She exhaled. "I knew it was my husband. So to save my life, I returned but without my daughter. I have been cooperative, acting all naive ever since with the hope that someday, I will reunite with my daughter," she said.

"You knew and experienced all this, and you could not warn me when I first came here? Because I was not your daughter?"

"Even if I wanted to, I could not trust a total stranger enough to spill the beans. I am truly sorry you are in this. But be subtle and wise if you wish to get out of this alive."

Footsteps interrupted us.

"Here they come." She raced to the door, unlocked it and hurried me out of her room. She whispered, "We never had this discussion."

I walked towards the footsteps, and bumped into my husband and father-in-law, probably searching for me.

"Hello, gentlemen," I said. "Honey, you took too long with father-in-law. C'mon, let us go." I slid between them and tugged Ade along.

Ade's father laughed hard and threw his hands in the air as a sign of surrender.

"Please, you may have your husband," he said and continued laughing as he walked towards his wife's room.

Slowly, Ade was back to himself. We had dinner and partied with his friends and colleagues occasionally. I even suggested once that I joined him at the hospital since I was a biochemist. He assured he will discuss that with his father.

Month grew into a year, he never did. I was too wise to make that a problem. So I used my unemployment to investigate him. I prowled through every document, books, shelves, drawers for any kind of proof, evidence or lead but found none.

Maybe I was over-exaggerating things. I fanned my face with my hand. The room had become too warm. I tapped my feet as I sat on the side of my bed. Then I felt a pull to the wardrobe top.

I opened the double door and by standing on a high stool, I reached a brief case and dragged it out. It fell to the floor. I jumped down from the stool to zip the case open, butterfly fluttering in my stomach. I rushed through the books inside.

There was *'The Books Of The Dark Shadow Angels'*.

I gasped for air, my palm clapped over my mouth. Then I laughed.

"Eureka! I have found it," I screamed.

Ade was one of the transforming angels.

I packed the books into the bag and returned the case to its spot, my heart pounding. I entered the kitchen and told my chef I had to prepare my husband's meal myself that evening.

Grinning as if I won a lottery, I prepared Ade's favourite sweet potatoes chicken soup, and served it nicely. I wore my sexiest lingerie, positioned my sexuality in an eye-catcher position and pretended to read a novel. A few minutes later, he returned home.

My trap caught a big whale.

He danced in just as I expected. "What are we celebrating today?"

He buried his head between my thighs. His tongue ran wild in there. I ran my hands down his shoulders, over the spine that lined his back. I moaned as he worked his thumb on my clit, before he pushed inside. He doubled with his index and middle finger, pumping faster, his tongue playing with my nipples.

I contracted my virginal muscles to delay my cuming, turned him over, I kissed his chest, abs and ran my tongue over his naval, down to his sack.

He groaned, "Shit!"

I squeezed his balls, sucked, throated it. I spat gummy saliva over his dick and ran my mouth over it.

He moaned. "Yes, so sweet. I'm cuming."

He bent me over, slid his dick in the doggy style and leaned over my back to fondle my breast. Faster and faster he went until we both came. We lay there spent, breathing hard.

I looked at his animated bony face and smiled. Once I know all your secrets and expose them, I am done with you, Ade.

He carried me to the dinning table. We ate, showered and spent the rest of the day in bed.

The following morning after he went off to work, I spent the day reading the brochure I found. I sometimes stopped breathing, shut my eyes to give my brain some room to process the content. These were similar rules but different practices from the one I read at Mike's library.

One chapter mentioned their 'ritual of wealth' was around the corner. Humans were sacrificed alive to the dark shadow Lord. And in return for wealth and prestige, each year, they must give a person for this ritual.

Am I his sacrificial lamb? My body turned hot and feverish. My skin became greyish green. Was it Ade's turn this time?

"Help me, dear mother." I paced, restless as a hen about to lay eggs.

Think, Bliss, think.

I marched to our wardrobe, ransacked it until I found a black bag tucked out of sight at the corner of one of the drawers. I swallowed a lump in my throat.

I unzipped the bag, dipped my hand in and pulled out a black cassock with a matching black balaclava, same as the pictures in the brochure.

My jaw dropped. I fell to my knees. Ade was fully prepared for the ritual of wealth.

I picked my handset and dialled Mike's number.

"Hello, Bliss, it has been a while. How are you?" Mike spoke on the other side of the line.

My voice shook as I said. "Do you still want custody of our son, little Mike?"

"Bliss? Is everything all right with you and Ade?"

"Do you want our son?" I asked again, trying to calm my nerves.

"Yes, of course, if it fine with you. I know your foster parents are nice people but I am his-"

I cut him off. "Then you can have him. I will ask Kennedy to get him ready so you can pick him over the weekend."

"Thank you, Bliss."

I cut the line. My lips trembled, but at least my son will be safe there. I sensed war approaching.

I staggered, holding on to the table to stand firm. When my head cleared a little, I took great care to arrange everything back in the wardrobe and the cassock bag in place. Shivering like a leave, I tugged myself into the sheet, turned the television to a cartoon network channel to distract me. I constantly thought about the hidden secrets and how I would uncover them all.

When Ade returned from work, he was all smiles with a bouquet of red roses. He placed a quick kiss on my forehead, the roses hidden behind, but partly showing from his weight line. He slowly pulled down the duvet, held me, and felt a rise in my temperature.

"Wow, you have a fever, honey," he said softly. "Have you taken any anti-malaria drugs or a aspirin?"

"Yes. I did and tucked myself in bed," I lied.

"Come to the table. The chef made us something delicious." He took my hands and led me out of bed.

After that day, I tried to take my mind off investigating more secrets. I called him to check on him at work, sent more romantic messages which ended us in more sexual exploration. Ade and I had agreed to spend the first five years of our marriage without kids, just enjoy ourselves and bond. So the thought of pregnancy was far from both our minds.

The only challenge was him not allowing me to work. Ade kicked against any idea to gain employment in his father's hospital or any other firm. So I slid back into the investigation to kill boredom and find answers.

Patiently, like a dog awaiting the butcher's bone, I observed his movements and checked daily to see if the black bag with the cassock had disappeared. Then my brother, Mike, visited without informing me, though they both seemed cool together.

His arrival brought fun to the house. Both himself and my husband, Ade had this wittiness that was captivating. They joked about everything, and put me in the centre as they bad-mouthed each other. Boys will always be boys, they say. It was so true for these two men.

Late in the evening, the two men lingered outside with a glass of scotch whisker, talking in deep tones.

Curious of their next moves, I called a taxi, same one I hired most times I did not wish to drive. I instructed him to stand guard and monitor any car that drove out of my compound and follow it to its destination. He would call and inform me when he had followed them to their stop. I paid him heavily.

He could not refuse. "Madam, if no be say the money big, I no for like do that kind risky business o," he said.

'That is all right. Thanks for accepting to do this for me."

Nothing happened that night. I paid him, but asked that he repeat a watch the next day. I was certain the ritual date on the brochure was a 19th.

Ade left for work the next morning. I told Mike I had to dash to the salon. Instead, I went searching for a cassock until I got something similar and a balaclava, too. Then I drove to the police station to file a complaint that my husband should be held responsible in case I turn up dead. After the officers guided me on how to go about the entrapment, I drove home ready.

I read through the terms and coded language in the brochure, memorized them until Mike's call interrupted me. I quickly put the book away and every other item that might implicate me. I had left the things I bought in the boot of my car.

"Why did you lock yourself inside your room, Mrs.?" Mike asked.

"I was tired, needed a little rest." I ran my hands over my eyes.

"I should have left you then, but we have not really spoken much since I arrived. I am leaving tonight," he said.

"Why leave at night, Mike?"

"Did your husband not tell you? We are going for a friend's house warming party. I will leave from there in the morning. It is an all night party."

"No, he did not. Does that mean I will come with you guys?" I smiled.

"Your husband will decide on that, Bliss. It is strictly for men." He put his hands on my neck to guide me towards the door. "Let us sit and talk about things, sister."

We walked to the sitting room.

"You know, Lisa still thinks you do not like her, Bliss."

I rose. "Mike! You interrupted my rest to talk about your wife, Lisa?' I do not care what she thinks." I turned away but he held my arm.

"I am not bringing this topic up for fun or to irritate you, sister. You two and our son are all I have got. Please, give her a chance."

"And she did not think twice when she told my husband about you being little Mike's father? What if what she did had destroyed my marriage? Let me warn you, Mike, if anything bad happen to our son, you and I will never see eye to eye forever."

"I apologise on her behalf. Please, forgive her, Bliss. She is taking good care of Little Mike," he assured.

"She better, Mike." I walked back to my room.

That evening, as scheduled, the taxi man positioned himself outside the gate, waiting to follow them. Ade showered, wore his cologne, a pair of jeans and tees on a sneakers. He smiled as he walked up to me.

"Honey, your brother and I are off to a party tonight. Sleep tight, we will be back in the morning."

"I will love to come along. Wait for me to get dressed." I jumped off the bed and headed to the wardrobe.

"I am sorry, it is an all-men-party. I promise to take you shopping tomorrow. Just name your price," he said

I pouted. "What a shame. They have missed what women offer at such parries." I slapped his ass and bit a side of my lips seductively.

"Do not turn me on, sweetheart. Just hang it there till am back, all right?"

"I will be dripping wet for you to come slut it in." I winked.

He giggled. "Naughty wifey. I love you just like that."

I peeped to see both of them walk to his car and drive out of the gate. I hurried to the wardrobe, but the black bag was missing. I wore my black gown and shoes. I could feel my blood pump faster than usual as my phone rang.

"Hello, madam, I follow them to where them stop for inside kio-kio village." The driver had successfully followed them to their stop.

"Thanks. Can you take me there? I will pay you twice the previous amount."

"Okay, I dey come pick you."

He drove me to a high-fenced hall.

"Madam na here o. Make I wait take you back?" he asked.

"No, you don't have to wait. I will find my way back home." I took my bag containing the items I bought earlier today and paid him his fees.

I stood there clueless on what to do next as the cab's light disappeared. I exhaled and threw on my cassock and balaclava over my face and walked to the gate.

I knocked.

A voice asked, "Ce tera gresa?"

I replied accordingly and the gate opened.

A man in black greeted me with a smile. "Ma, you are late. The ritual has started. Good thing is, the Lord has not yet descended. Hurry!"

I walked fast along the long corridor, trying not to appear lost. Everywhere was quiet till I approached the entrance of the long hall then I heard the moan of female voices. I stepped into the open hall divided by a see-through glass wall. An aesthetic blue light in the hall illuminated more than fifteen naked women with balaclava over their head. A man stood in their middle; and they all shared him, crawling over him, sucking, kissing, as if they were possessed. They did not notice my presence.

I stood staring and forgot to take off my cassock in order to blend in.

A deep voice whispered in my ear. "What do you think you are doing there?"

The hairs on my neck stood, my knees weakened. The voice sounded like my father-in-law's. I tried to speak, but only a faint whimper emerged. The man dragged me through the pathway, tore off my cassock and flung my balaclava away. My hair fell over my face and spread around my neck.

"Take your clothes off now," he ordered.

My legs wobbled. I struggled out of my garments.

"Since you are here, we might as well offer you as extra," he said in a hoarse voice. His face remained hidden under the mask, but I could tell from his physique, he was Ade's father.

He dragged me to the side of the hall where I had seen the men through the glass divider wall. The stringent smell of cum and arousal fluid mixed with sweat filled the blue-lighted hall. A weak, naked young girl was positioned between the knees of one of the men. I saw fear written all over her face.

She screamed as they tossed her around the hall and fucked her in turns. Her tears meant nothing to the monsters. Fear gripped me. I struggled to speak.

"Please, don't do this to me. I beg you," I cried.

The man, who had the figure of my father-in-law, tossed me into the mix. The first man grabbed me, bent me over and thrust into me. I screamed. He bit me in his pleasure, groaning like a zombie. He slapped my face, fucked harder as I wept. He pulled out and released his semen into a chalice, and then tossed me over to the next person, who grabbed my arms and forced them backward. He chewed on my nipples like a wild hungry dog.

I screamed as the man pushed his fingers inside me. He fingered my cunt insanely, his nails piercing my virginal wall. I yelled as they took turns torturing both the girl and I to their pleasure.

Then, one of them held me. From his breath, I believed he was my father. His hands trembled as he touched me. I heard his teeth grind. He pushed me to my husband, Ade. His cologne gave him away. He oozed Armani Code.

Ade hugged me tight. He moaned in pain more than in pleasure, then he thrust in and came into the chalice just as the others did. He passed me to another, who I presumed was Mike. I was too weak to cry. I felt nothing. I wanted to die.

But he called softly, "Bliss, please, do not give up so soon."

His voice brought back a little hope that I might leave here alive. He thrust his dick into me and stayed still. He held me to his chest, his arms around me. Then the girl's high-pitched scream rang out again. I looked up to see the girl laid on the altar at the centre of the hall,

My heart thundered. Too weak to move, she laid motionless as if already dead. She must have been in her twenties because she looked young.

Few seconds later, a voice roared. A dark shadow crawled over her, she trembled, convulsed and gave up.

My eyes popped out from their sockets. I was next. The man, who brought me into the mix, pulled my hair, detached me from Mike. He made me climb on the altar, but a man, who looked like my father, put himself on the platform instead. The loud voice roared again and there were commotion in the hall.

One of the men grabbed me off the altar and carried me on his shoulders. He ran out to the car pack, loud alarm bells dogged his footsteps. At the gate, he spoke some strange language to the man in a horrified tone. The man opened the gate, and he drove the fastest I had ever been driven.

"Bliss, it me, Mike! Where should I take you?"

"Pastor Akpan's church in Akwa Ibom."

He drove till dawn. Under my directives, we arrived at the church. He pulled off his tee-shirts and put it over me to cover myself up.

"Bliss, run as far as you can," he said and drove away.

I staggered into the church building, pushed the door open, and crawled to the altar.

I passed out.

In the vision, a dark shadow hovered on the church ceiling. Long, thick and dark. It crawled towards me at the altar. I tried to run but my legs felt lifeless. My eyes remained on this horrid apparition as it crawled towards me. A bright light appeared. It twinkled and overshadowed the darkness, and swallowed it up.

I regained consciousness and opened my eyes.

I was still on the altar of the church, surrounded by the church prayer band members and Pastor Akpan. They were praying in tongues.

"She is alive. She has regained consciousness."

I looked down. They had covered my waist to my feet with a *wrapper*, where the shirt didn't cover.

"Who are you?" one of the women asked.

"She is Blissful, one of us," Pastor Akpan replied. "The battle is over for you, my daughter."

I looked at him. "Yes, the supernatural light has conquered the supernatural darkness."

"Let that be your reality from today," the women chorused.

That was my reality, twisted, but the light won.

My reality had just begun. It is a TWISTED REALITY.